# Death of
# a Mystery Writer

# ROBERT BARNARD

# Death of a Mystery Writer

CHARLES SCRIBNER'S SONS
NEW YORK

First U.S. edition published by Charles Scribner's Sons, 1979

Copyright © 1978 Robert Barnard

Library of Congress Cataloging in Publication Data

Barnard, Robert.
   Death of a mystery writer.

   First published in Great Britain in 1978 under title: Unruly son.
   I.   Title.
PZ4.B25877Dc 1979 [PR6052.A665]     823'.9'14     79-12090
ISBN 0-684-16280-6

1 3 5 7 9 11 13 15 17 19  F/C  20 18 16 14 12 10 8 6 4 2

Printed in the United States of America

# CONTENTS

| | | |
|---|---|---|
| I | THE UNPLEASANTNESS AT THE PRINCE ALBERT | 7 |
| II | OLIVER FAIRLEIGH'S WEEK | 11 |
| III | OLIVER FAIRLEIGH'S WEEK (TWO) | 23 |
| IV | OLIVER FAIRLEIGH'S SATURDAY | 34 |
| V | SUDDENLY AT HIS RESIDENCE | 46 |
| VI | MOURNED BY HIS FAMILY ... | 59 |
| VII | SAID THE PIGGY: I WILL | 65 |
| VIII | STRONG POISON | 75 |
| IX | FATHER AND SON | 89 |
| X | MASTER AND MAN | 99 |
| XI | BARABBAS | 109 |
| XII | SOMETHING UNSPOKEN | 120 |
| XIII | DE MORTUIS ... | 132 |
| XIV | DOWNSTAIRS, UPSTAIRS | 143 |
| XV | BLACK SHEEP | 155 |
| XVI | TERMINAL | 169 |
| XVII | DEATH COMES AS THE END | 176 |

### CHAPTER I

## The Unpleasantness at the Prince Albert

It was saturday night, and the saloon bar of the Prince Albert was nicely full: there was plump, jolly Mrs Corbett from the new estate, whose laugh – gurgling with gin and tonic – periodically rang through the whole pub; there was her husband, her teenage daughter looking bored and her old mother looking daggers – all on a family night out; at other tables there were would-be-smooth young men and their silly girl-friends, fat men with fishing stories and thin men with fishy handshakes, and in the corner there was the inevitable sandy-haired man on his own, with his single whisky and his evening paper.

From the public bar came the dull, horrendous thud of the juke box, concession to a civilization in decline; but on good nights the saloon bar could make enough noise to forget it, and tonight was a good night: Jim Turner, the publican, had early cottoned on to the fact that nobody cares any more about the quality of beer in a pub, and that all they are interested in is pub food. Thus, on a Friday and Saturday night he did a roaring trade in pies, plates of beef and turkey, scotch eggs and sizzling sausages – all washed down with a brew that looked like dandelion juice and tasted like poodle's urine.

'Here's a nice bit of breast for you, sir,' he would say, bustling up with a plate, 'and I can't say fairer than that, can I?'

Around the bar stood little groups of men and their wives and ladies, telling stories and waiting to tell stories. But at the end of the bar, nearly squeezed into a corner, was one solitary young man, his eyes concentrated on his pint mug. He was quite well-dressed in his way: his dark suit was new, almost sharp, his shirt good quality, though not very clean. He was good-looking in his way, too, but it was not a very well-defined way: his lips were full, but self-indulgent, without line or determination; his cheeks were unfurrowed, almost hairless, and his eyes were large and liquid – so large and liquid that he seemed as he stood there to be near to tears of self-pity.

He was, in fact, rather drunk. This was his fourth pint of best bitter, and though it was not very good he had declined Jim Turner's suggestion that he go on to stronger stuff. His trips to the lavatory had become frequent, and last time he had nearly knocked over Mrs Corbett's glass, and had been given a piece of that lady's tongue. He talked to no one, read no paper: he merely stood or sat on his stool, contemplating his glass as if it were his *curriculum vitae*. Now and then he smoked – nervously, carelessly, and always stubbing out the cigarette before he was half-way through it.

At the nearest table to him a local couple from Hadley had met up with 'foreigners' from Bracken. Bracken was a new town, thirty-five miles away. It was full of Londoners and Northerners, all of whom could be treated with friendly contempt by locals when they motored out of their brick and glass elysium and stopped for the evening at a real pub. Tonight Jack and Doris were doing the honours of the vicinity, and Ted and Vera from Bracken were being quiet and humble.

' 'Course, a lot of the old places have been bought up for cottages,' said Doris, 'places I knew when I was a girl, real run down and awful – well, they've been bought up, by outsiders, you know, and you wouldn't believe the prices!'

'Lot of well-known people, too,' said Jack, 'because we're still pretty convenient for London. There's that Penny Feather, for example, the actress – '

'I don't think I've – '

' 'Course you have. You know: "Why is your hair so soft and shiny, Mummy?" She does the mummy.'

'Oh yes, I – '

''Course you have. Well, she's got a cottage just down the road. Comes down at weekends. Real smasher. Comes in here sometimes, with different men. You do see life here, I can tell you. Specially on a Saturday night.'

'Then there's Arnold Silver – *Sir* Arnold, I beg his pardon.'

'The financier?'

'That's it. Got it in one. Always bringing libel actions. *He* bought the Old Manor. Wife sometimes lives there weeks on end. He's just down here now and again, of course.'

'We don't see *them* – they're never in here. Pity, really. We could ask him for a good tip for the Stock Market.' Everyone laughed jollily and drank up.

'Then,' said Doris, 'not in Hadley, but in Wycherley – that's twelve miles south on the London road – in Wycherley there's Oliver Fairleigh.'

She paused, and gazed complacently down at her navy two-piece, knowing that Ted and Vera would need no prompting over the significance of this name.

'Really?' said Ted, decidedly impressed. 'I didn't know he lived around here.'

'Just outside Wycherley,' said Jack. 'It was the old squire's house, but the family went to pieces after the war. He's lived there twenty-odd years now.'

'I like a good thriller,' said Ted.

'He's *ingenious* with it,' said Doris, not quite sure this was the right description.

'Yes, they're more detective stories, aren't they? People buy them, though, don't they?'

'He's top of the best-sellers every Christmas,' said Doris, now swelling with vicarious author's pride. She did not notice, by the bar, that Jim Turner was giving significant (and obsequious) grins at the young drunk man in the corner.

'I've heard he's a bit of a tartar,' said Ted. Jack and

Doris were rather unsure whether it added more to the prestige of the neighbourhood if he was or if he wasn't a tartar.

'Can't believe all you read in the papers,' said Jack.

'Well, he *is*, that's true,' said Doris. 'But he *is* an author. It's different, somehow, isn't it?'

'I suppose so,' said Vera, not quite convinced.

'And he's had his troubles,' said Jack, lowering his voice, but only by a fraction.

'Oh?'

'From his family,' said Doris, who had never set eyes on any of them. 'You know how it is. They've not turned out well.' She shook her head enigmatically.

'Well, there's one boy,' said Jack, 'plays with a pop group.'

'There's a lot of money to be made wi' them groups,' said Ted.

'It's not *that* good. And it doesn't go well with the image: his real name is Sir Oliver Fairleigh-Stubbs, you know, with the hyphen, and he's always been very country squire. The children had nannies and all that – everything the best and no expense spared. Anyway, it's not just him – the girl's very wild they say – '

'And the eldest boy, well, he really has been a case,' said Jack, quite unconscious of the fact that behind him Jim Turner's face was creased in anguish and he was trying to get one of his other customers to dig him in the ribs.

'Drifted from job to job,' said Doris, 'never held one down more than six months.'

'Debts here there and everywhere,' said Jack, 'and not a matter of five or ten pounds either, believe you me. His father had to foot them, of course.'

'Had the police up there once,' said Doris.

'It's the mother I feel sorry for.'

'He's a hopeless case, they say – a real ne'er-do-well. Still, it's often the way, isn't it?'

'It makes you think, though, doesn't it? A young chap like that, with everything going for him.'

They were interrupted by the crash of an overturning bar-stool. The young man from the corner lunged in their direction, paused unsteadily in mid-lunge, and then came to rest with both hands on their table, gazing – red, blotchy and bleary – into their eyes.

'He had everything going for him, did he? Well, he had his father going for him twenty-four hours a day, that's true enough.' He gulped, his speech became still more slurred, and the lakes that were his eyes at last overflowed. 'You don't know what . . . You don't know what you're talking about. You never met my . . . my famous father. If you had you'd know he was a . . . *swine*. He's a bastard. He's the biggest goddam bastard that ever walked this . . . bloody earth.' He turned to stand up and make a pronouncement to the whole bar, but he failed to make the perpendicular, and crashed back on to the table.

'My father ought to be shot,' he sobbed.

<br>

### CHAPTER II

## OLIVER FAIRLEIGH'S WEEK

*Sunday*

SIR OLIVER FAIRLEIGH-STUBBS sat in the back seat of his Daimler, surveying the world through bulbous, piggy eyes. Over his knees, and over those of his wife who sat beside him, was a rug, although it was June and the sun was shining. Sir Oliver, though still enough to the casual glance, was far from asleep. His eyes were noticing everything, and sometimes sparkling as if in anticipation. From time to time he pursed his mouth up, or blew out his cheeks; at others he let out little grunts, like a sow in ecstasy.

Lady Fairleigh-Stubbs knew the signs, and sighed. Oliver was intending to be difficult. Perhaps to make a scene. Against her better judgement (for she knew that nothing she said was likely to have any effect on her husband's behaviour, except to make it worse) she said:

'Such a nice couple, the Woodstocks.'

'Who?' or rather an interrogatory grunt, was the reply.

'The Woodstocks. And charming of them to invite us to lunch.'

The grunt, this time, was just a grunt.

'They're poor as church-mice,' said Lady Fairleigh-Stubbs.

'Must want something,' said her husband.

'So brave, to set out on a writing career at the moment, when things are so difficult.'

'Not brave, bloody ridiculous,' said Sir Oliver. 'Deserves to land himself in the poor-house, if by the grace of God we still had them.'

He puffed out his cheeks to give himself an expression of outrage. Lady Fairleigh-Stubbs sighed again.

'Drive slower!' barked Sir Oliver suddenly to Surtees, the chauffeur. 'I want to look at the trees.' As the car slowed down, he let his great treble chin flop on to his chest, and closed his eyes.

'Oliver, we're here,' said his wife – a thing he knew perfectly well. He opened his eyes wide, and surveyed the landscape as if he had just got off an international flight.

'Not *that*,' he said, as the Daimler pulled up at a wicket-gate. 'Good God, I thought artists' cottages went out in my youth.'

'They've knocked two together and done them up,' said Lady Fairleigh-Stubbs, as if that excused the decidedly twee effect. 'I think it's awfully pretty. I gather this is one of the few bits of property the Woodstocks have left.'

When Surtees came round to open the door, Oliver Fairleigh remained seated in the car for a full minute, his hands spanning his monstrous tummy, gazing with distaste at the orange-painted cottage, and knowing perfectly well he was being observed from inside. Then he climbed puffily out and stood by the gate. When the front

door opened – the minimum acknowledgement that he
was looked for – he condescended to open the gate himself.

'You've got no hollyhocks!' he bellowed to the young
couple in the doorway.

'I beg your pardon . . . ?'

'You've got no hollyhocks,' he repeated, at twice the
volume. 'Cottages like this have to have hollyhocks.' He
gave his arm to his wife and stumped into the house – past
his hosts and straight into the living-room.

'Eleanor!' said a washed-out-looking lady by the fireplace, coming forward to kiss her, 'So good of you to come.
And Oliver! How well you're looking.'

Oliver Fairleigh-Stubbs surveyed the elder Mrs Woodstock. Her gentility, like the colours of her woollens, seemed
not to have been fast, and to have come out in the wash. 'I
have got gout, impetigo and athlete's foot,' he announced,
'but no doubt to the casual observer I look well.' He sank
into the best armchair and looked ahead, as if contemplating mankind's extinction with gloomy relish.

'Harold Drayton you've met,' said Mrs Woodstock
vaguely. Oliver Fairleigh grunted. Harold Drayton was a
walking gentleman, a tame nobody who could be counted
on to make up a lunch-party, one who valued a reasonable
meal more than he disliked the company of Oliver
Fairleigh (there were few such). He was worth, in the
estimation of the guest of honour, no more than a faint
grunt.

By this time the host and hostess were back in the room,
having been exchanging glances in the tiny kitchen.
Benjamin Woodstock was tall and willowy in the Rupert
Brooke manner, though without the good looks. In fact, like
his mother, he looked indefinably mangy. Celia his wife
was, at that moment, looking frankly terrified.

However, with the offer of sherry, Oliver Fairleigh's
mood changed. He sat back in his chair, beaming in his
porcine way at all and sundry, and responding to con-
versational advances. His voice, something between a

public-school sports-master's and a sergeant-major's, was not adapted to polite conversation, but nevertheless everyone in the room began to relax a little – except Eleanor his wife, who knew him too well.

'They tell me you write, eh?' boomed Sir Oliver, baring his teeth at Ben Woodstock.

'Well, yes, just a little,' said Ben. Then, thinking this did not sound too good in view of his purpose in inviting the great Oliver Fairleigh, he added: 'But I'm hoping to make a living out of it.'

Oliver Fairleigh left, for him, quite a short pause. 'Oh yes? What at? Eh?'

'Well, I've just had a detective story accepted.'

Oliver Fairleigh snorted. 'Detective stories? No money in them. You'll starve in six months. Write a thriller.'

'Oh, do you think so?'

'Write a thriller. One of those documentaries. Somebody trying to shoot the Pope – that kind of nonsense. Fill it full of technical details. Those are the things people buy these days.'

'I'm not sure about the technical details – I don't think I'd be too good on them.'

'Make 'em up, dear boy, make 'em up. Only one in a hundred knows any better, and he won't bother to write and correct you. You'll never get anywhere if you over-estimate your public.'

'Trying to shoot the Pope. That does sound a good idea,' said the elder Mrs Woodstock meditatively. Oliver Fairleigh turned to her urbanely.

'Ah – you feel strongly about birth-control, I suppose?' He looked at her in a frankly appraising way, and then laughed.

This comparatively bright mood lasted Sir Oliver just into lunch, as his wife knew it would. Such a mood was never to be trusted, and was the prelude to (and was intended to contrast with) some other mood or series of moods which would be launched on his companions' lulled sensibilities.

The fish was a very uninteresting little bit of plaice, hardly able to support the circlet of lemon on top. Everyone went at it as if fish were a duty which there was no point in trying to make into a pleasure. Not so Oliver Fairleigh. He gazed at it with a beam of anticipation, then set about masticating it with an elaborate pantomime of savouring every succulent mouthful. He devoted himself to the miserable triangle of nutriment with all the zest due to a classic French dish. Periodically he wiped his mouth and beamed with simulated enthusiasm round the table, as if to ensure that the other guests were properly appreciating the gastronomic distinction of it. They looked at him in dubious acknowledgement of his sunny temper. His wife looked at her plate.

Over the crumbed cutlet that followed a new performance was enacted. Oliver Fairleigh sank into a mood of intense depression: he gazed at the cutlet as if it were a drowned friend whose remains he was trying to identify at a police morgue. He picked up a forkful of mashed potato, inspected it, smelt it, and finally, with ludicrously overdone reluctance, let it drop into his mouth, where he chewed it for fully three minutes before swallowing. Conversation flagged.

It was the wine Ben Woodstock was worried about. Oliver Fairleigh was acknowledged a connoisseur of wine: every other book he wrote was studded with some item of wine lore or some devastating judgement designed to wither the ignorant. He was consulted by experts, and had been quoted by Cyril Ray. As he took up his glass, Ben's heart sank. It wouldn't be right. In spite of all the advice he'd had, all the money he'd spent, it wouldn't be right.

Sir Oliver looked, frowned, sipped, frowned, set down his glass and stared ahead of him in gloomy silence. Once or twice he made as if to say something to his host (sitting beside him, and looking more meagre than ever) but each time he stopped himself, as if he had had second thoughts. Finally he took up his glass and downed the contents in one go.

Over the pudding – something spongy, which had gone soggy – Ben Woodstock felt the weight of the silence had become too heavy to bear, and began once to make conversation with his guest of honour.

'I suppose you find it's very important to establish some kind of routine when you're writing, don't you, sir?'

'Eh? What? What do I find important?'

'Routine.'

'Who says I find routine important?'

'I said I *suppose* you find routine important in writing.'

'Oh. You suppose, do you? Hmm.'

The silence continued until the pudding had been eaten, when Ben tried again.

'I was wondering if you could give me any advice – '

'Eh?'

'I was wondering if you could give me any advice – '

'Sack your cook,' said Oliver Fairleigh-Stubbs in a voice of thunder that silenced all the lesser voices around the table. 'Best piece of advice I can give you.'

Celia Woodstock got up and darted towards the kitchen in the fearsome silence that followed. Then they all adjourned for coffee. Having made a scene, Oliver Fairleigh was for the moment peaceful. Ben Woodstock noticed the change of mood, and knowing the reputation for brevity of his guest's good tempers, he felt he had to take advantage of it. Greatly daring, in view of the quality of the coffee, he approached the subject which the meal had been intended to lead up to.

'I was wondering about publishers, sir – '

Oliver Fairleigh fixed him with a stare. 'Thought you'd got a book accepted,' he said.

'Well yes, I have, actually. By Robinson and Heath.' The firm in question was tiny, and of no repute. Oliver Fairleigh grunted. 'Of course I'm terribly grateful to them, taking a chance on an unknown author, and all that, but naturally I'm thinking a little of the future too. I know you're a Macpherson's author yourself, and I was wondering – '

'Quite exceptionally good firm, Robinson and Heath,' interrupted Oliver Fairleigh with unusual energy. 'You're in really good hands there. Nothing like these small firms for taking care of you. Keep out of the hands of the big boys. Never know where you are with all these amalgamations. Next thing you know you're being paid in dollars or Saudi Arabian yashmaks or God knows what. No, stick to Robinson and Heath, my boy. You're in real luck if you're in with them.'

He rose, panting and snorting, to his feet. 'Come, Eleanor, we must be off.' He made for the door, and accepted gracefully the ritual gestures made to a departing guest. 'So nice to have a meal with old friends,' he boomed. 'Goodbye Mr – er – er – ' and he gazed at Harold Drayton for a moment, as though trying to think of a reason for his existence, bared his teeth at the elder Mrs Woodstock, and then sailed out through the door. As he shook hands with his young host and hostess he grunted his thanks, and then fixed the luckless Ben with an eye of outrage.

'One thing I wanted to say, my boy,' he said, in his voice of thunder. 'That wine, that wine you served. It was . . .' the pause ran on, and on, and Ben Woodstock remained transfixed by that terrible eye, unable to stir a muscle . . . 'very good,' concluded Oliver Fairleigh. 'Quite exceptionally fine. Come to dinner with me next Saturday, eh? You and your wife? We'll expect you.'

And he turned and made off to his car.

As they drove home, Sir Oliver folded his hands once more over his ballooning stomach, shook now and then in delighted self-appreciation and stole glances at his wife out of the corner of his eye.

'I'm glad I told that lie about the appalling wine,' he said finally. 'It does one good, once in a way, to make simple people happy.'

*Monday*
Oliver Fairleigh-Stubbs sat in his study, glaring resentfully at a glass of water on the table by his side. At his feet

sat his boxer dog, Cuff, grunting periodically. In this and in other respects Cuff resembled his master, and had in fact been acquired with a view to his providing a canine variation on the Oliver Fairleigh theme. So he grunted, snuffled, snapped periodically at inoffensive callers, and generally gave people to comment on the well-known idea that dogs grow like their owners. Which was unfair, for taken by and large Cuff was a harmless animal.

Oliver Fairleigh was dictating, in his over-loud voice, the last chapter of his latest detective story. It was one of his Inspector Powys ones, and it had to be with his publishers before the week was out, if they were to make the Christmas market.

' "The thing that nobody has remarked," said Inspector Powys, wagging an admonitory finger at his fascinated audience, "is the curious position of the body. Now, Mrs Edwards was cutting bread, look you – " ' Oliver Fairleigh paused. 'Have we had a "look you" in the last three pages, Miss Cozzens?'

Barbara Cozzens (whose efficiency was such that she could take perfect shorthand while her thoughts were miles away) flicked irritatedly through her notebook. 'I don't think so, Sir Oliver.'

'People get annoyed if there are too many and annoyed if there are none at all,' said Oliver Fairleigh, testily. 'Personally I've no idea whether the Welsh say it or not. Do they, Miss Cozzens?'

'All the Welsh people I know are very Anglicized,' said Barbara Cozzens distantly, adding rather acidly: 'It's a bit late in the day to start worrying about that.'

'True, true. I'm stuck with it now, just as I'm stuck with the over-sexed little Welsh idiot who says it. Where were we? "Mrs Edwards was cutting bread, look you, to take upstairs for the family tea. Now to cut bread – you perhaps would not be aware of this, Lord Fernihill, but I assure you it is so – the body must lean *forward*. Many a time I've watched my old mother doing it, God rest her soul. Now Mrs Edwards was a heavy woman, and she was stabbed from behind – and yet she fell *backwards*. Now . . ." '

For the next hour Miss Cozzens let her thoughts wander. When she had first come to work for Oliver Fairleigh she had followed his works with interest, had been eager to hear the solution, and had once pointed out a flaw in Inspector Powys's logic. But only once. Sir Oliver had fixed her with his gob-stopper eye and said: 'Any fool could see that. But my readers won't.' And he had gone on dictating, unperturbed. That was a long time ago. Then Miss Cozzens had often read detective stories for pleasure; now she shied away from them at station bookstalls, and hated the sound of the name Powys. She sat there, upright, her hand making dancing patterns over the paper, her mind full of Amalfi last summer, the widower who had made advances to her there, and the sensitive novel she was writing about the episode – a fragile, delicate story, gossamer light, every adjective chosen with loving care and Roget's Thesaurus.

'"And as Inspector Powys drove back along the stately drive to Everton Lodge, he shook his head at the pity of it, and smiled his sad, compassionate smile. THE END." That's it. Thank God I've done with that Welsh twit for another year or two. Next time it will be a Mrs Merrydale murder. Or I'll just have a common or garden policeman. A drink, I think, Miss Cozzens.'

'The doctor – '

'Damn the doctor,' roared Sir Oliver, kicking Cuff to make him growl in sympathy. 'I don't take orders from any quack. I don't get shot of Inspector Powys every day of the week. Now, unlock the bottom drawer, there's a good girl, and we'll both have a glass of sherry. You know where the glasses are.'

With a sigh Miss Cozzens complied. If Sir Oliver was going to start this sort of thing regularly, he'd be well on the way to killing himself. At least nobody could say she hadn't warned him. She found the concealed bottle, got two glasses from the cupboard, and poured two not-quite-full glasses.

'Full!' roared Oliver Fairleigh, like a baby in a paddy.
Cuff got laboriously to his feet and growled at her in an
ugly manner. Miss Cozzens, with another sigh, filled her
employer's glass, and – after a moment's thought – her
own too. Then all three of them settled down to a rather
frosty celebration.

'Did you enjoy the book, Miss Cozzens?' enquired Sir
Oliver Fairleigh-Stubbs, after his first sip.

'I beg your pardon?'

'The book, Miss Cozzens. The masterwork that we have
been working on together.'

'I'm afraid I haven't been paying much attention, Sir
Oliver. I'm sure it will do very well.'

'Of course it will do very well,' said Sir Oliver testily.
'Other people like my books, even if you do not.' He
softened under the influence of the sherry. 'You're quite
right, though. They're very bad. And especially the
Inspector Powys ones. They are quite beneath me.
Perhaps I won't write any more. Get myself a new
detective. Someone who's a gentleman.'

'I believe the trend is all the other way these days,'
observed Miss Cozzens.

'I SET MY OWN TRENDS!' roared Oliver Fairleigh.
He impressed Cuff, but Miss Cozzens declined to jump,
and went on calmly sipping her sherry. 'The best thing,'
went on Sir Oliver, as if he had never raised his voice,
'would be to write just one more, and kill the little beast
off in the course of it.'

Miss Cozzens nodded her approval. '*Inspector Powys's
Last Case*,' she said. 'I'm sure you could think of a good
way to get rid of him. Something lingering with boiling
oil in it would be nice.' She found her spirits rising already
at the very thought.

'Absolutely,' agreed Sir Oliver. 'There's a project we
might both enjoy collaborating on. It would cause a
great sensation.'

'People would be desolated. The letters would flow in.'

'Exactly,' said Sir Oliver. 'The lights would go out all

over Wales.' He considered the prospect benignly for some minutes further. Then the practical sense which had gained him his present position and kept him there reasserted itself. 'And if the new man didn't catch on,' he said, 'after a few years we could somehow or other bring Powys to life again.'

Miss Cozzens's spirits sank.

*Tuesday*

Sir Oliver Fairleigh-Stubbs was assisted into the BBC studio by the producer. He did not normally need assistance when he walked. Sixty-five years, and habits of self-indulgence, had left him less than spry, but he did manage to get around on his own, with a good deal of puffing and blowing. On the other hand, it was a common practice of his to lull his victims into a false sense of security, whether by an assumed geniality or by putting up a pretence of being but a shadow of his former self.

He's a shadow of his former self, thought the producer to himself, with relief.

A show of geniality would not have worked at the BBC. His brushes with that institution had been too many. He had disrupted innumerable talk-programmes, driven the audience of *Any Questions* to throw West Country farm produce at the stage, turned on inoffensive interviewers with accusations of communism (the more embarrassing since most of them were prospective candidates in the Conservative or Liberal interests). No. Geniality would cut no ice at the BBC.

Today Oliver Fairleigh was to broadcast for *The Sunday Appeal* and the producer congratulated himself that nothing could go radically wrong. He would be alone with his script, with no one to antagonize or be antagonized by. He led him to the table, sat him comfortably in the chair, and drew his attention to the glass of water placed at his right hand.

Oliver Fairleigh sat still as a gargoyle on a waterspout, staring beadily at the microphone while the technical preparations went on around him. Finally the producer smiled ingratiatingly.

'If we might just test for voice, Sir Oliver . . . ?'

Oliver Fairleigh cleared his throat with a bellow, and began:

'I am speaking to you today on behalf of the Crime Writers' Benevolent Association . . .'

The producer nodded his head in appreciation. It was an admirable radio voice, rich, resonant, redolent of pheasant, port wine, and good living in general.

'Right,' he said, 'I think we can go ahead.' And at a signal from him, Oliver Fairleigh began again.

'I am speaking to you today on behalf of the Crime Writers' Benevolent Association,' he said. 'I have no doubt there are few among you who have not at one time or another whiled away the tedium of your summer holidays with a detective story.' The producer smiled sycophantically. It was a good script as these things went – different, made people sit up. 'I leave it to the sociologists to explain the fascination of crime stories for the public at large – as no doubt they can do, at least to their own satisfaction. For myself I have no idea whether we incite people to crime, or deflect the impulse they feel to commit it, and it is not germane to my purpose today, which is quite different: it is, quite frankly, to ask you to put your hands in your pockets. The Crime Writers' Benevolent Association – which I might describe as a very harmless sort of trade union – has acquired a large country house in a non-violent part of rural England, and aims (if public support is forthcoming) to set up a home there for elderly and infirm writers of crime fiction.'

Still gazing intently at his script, Oliver Fairleigh went on:

'Picture to yourselves the condition of these poor hacks, whose mastery of their miserable trade is so uncertain that they have proved unable to provide for themselves a comfortable autumn to their lives.' The producer looked at the technician, and the technician looked at the producer but Oliver Fairleigh, apparently oblivious, continued gazing at his script. 'Picture to yourselves the condition of mental debility to which a lifetime of locked-room murders, rigged alibis and poisons unknown to medical science has reduced them. Imagine them in their final days quoting to each other the feeble catch-phrases of their fictional sleuths. If such a picture of mental and physical decay does not evoke from you feelings of benevolence, then you are, I fear, beyond the reach of calls upon your Christian charity. Good night to you all.'

As the technician switched off the tape, the producer got up, wringing his hands, with a wide smile on his face.

'That was most amusing, Sir Oliver. If we could record the last paragraph again, as it stands in the script – '

'Script!' bellowed Oliver Fairleigh, pushing back his chair and making for the door with an astonishing speed and agility. 'I've been reading the script. Must have sent you an early draft. Take it or leave it, my dear chap. Take it or leave it.'

And he disappeared out of the studio in the direction of the lifts.

The producer sank back into his chair, looking very depressed.

'I suppose I'd better get on to Dick Francis,' he said.

CHAPTER III

OLIVER FAIRLEIGH'S WEEK (TWO)

*Wednesday*

OLIVER FAIRLEIGH had arranged to meet his daughter at Manrico's, a restaurant on the less seedy outer fringe of Soho where he knew the food would be up to his requirements. He did not meet her at any of his more usual haunts because he was afraid she would turn up in patched denim and raucous check.

As it was, Bella turned up crisp and delectable in ravishingly close-fitting shirt and slacks which cried aloud of fashion and expense. The faces of middle-rank executives, pink from expense-account wine, swivelled at her entrance and followed her greedily and regretfully until she seated herself opposite her father. Bella, when she wanted to, could epitomize style and breeding, and use both qualities to add to her desirability. She had beauty, of a slightly pixie quality, she had a glorious mass of auburn hair, she had a body which moved confidently knowing it would be admired and that a chair would be there when she sat down. Bella was Oliver Fairleigh's favourite child. Indeed, she was the only one he liked at all.

Over the antipasti Bella looked at her father – that hoydenish look that made strong men grovel – and said: 'What's this I hear about you at the BBC?'

Oliver Fairleigh, biting on an olive, burst into a great wheezy chuckle of delight, which turned into a choke.

'How did you hear of that?' he asked.

'We in the newspaper world hear everything – you should know that by now,' said Bella.

'Newspaper world!' snorted Oliver Fairleigh. 'A gang of pimps and informers! A fine crowd for my daughter to mix with.' He paused, and then it was his turn to look roguish. 'Anyway I should hardly think the *Gardening Gazette* deserves to be dignified with the title of newspaper.'

'It's a start,' said Bella, shrugging with indifference. 'One makes contacts.'

'Hmmm,' said Oliver Fairleigh, looking displeased. 'I suppose that means you're sleeping around with the editors.'

'The editors, Daddy, are far too old to be interested,' said Bella. 'And anyway, they keep such peculiar hours.' Oliver Fairleigh looked far from satisfied with this answer. 'But the BBC,' said Bella, noting his mood. 'What exactly did you *do*?'

A great wicked grin spread over Oliver Fairleigh's face. 'I wrote a new script. I'll give it to you if you like. You should have seen the producer's face. He's been hearing these bromides week after week, and suddenly I pumped an enema into him!' The great wheezy chuckle emerged again, pushing itself out like reluctantly emitted wind. It stopped short when the wine waiter appeared at his elbow. Oliver Fairleigh was never frivolous about wine.

'Are you allowed to drink?' asked Bella suspiciously.

'Wine, yes. Not anything stronger, except at weekends. But a little wine, oh yes, certainly.'

'For your stomach's sake, I suppose.'

Oliver Fairleigh gazed with comic dismay at that great protuberance. 'Well, it would certainly play up if it were denied it,' he said. 'Whisky it can do without: a vulgar, provincial tipple. Even liqueurs it can deny itself. But wine – it would be the height of idiocy to deny oneself wine merely to live a little longer.'

When he had tasted the selected bottle, Oliver Fairleigh nodded his head, and settled down to enjoy his meal, muttering as he did so: 'I'm not satisfied about you and those editors!'

'How odd,' said his daughter, 'that good wine never puts you in a good mood.'

'Why should it?' growled Oliver Fairleigh. 'Good wine should be taken as a matter of course. Superlative wine might put me in a good mood. Bad wine certainly puts me in a bad one. Bad wine like that fool Woodstock's.'

'Woodstock? Do you mean Ben Woodstock?'

'Some such name.'

'I didn't know he was back in Wycherley.'

'Living in a damnfool artist's cottage. Looks as if he expects Henry James to drop by any minute and swap ambiguities with him. But he got me instead.' He pursed out his lips in delighted remembrance of the occasion.

'Poor Ben,' said Bella, watching him closely. 'I suppose you scared the living daylights out of him. You used to when he was a boy.'

'I think,' said her father, 'that they'd do a term in the prisons of President Amin rather than go through that again.'

'Oh Daddy, you *are* appalling. You're a monster. Why do you do it?'

Oliver put on a pout, looked like an overfed baby, and said: 'I get bored. I have to have things happening. Don't be hard on me, Bella. You should understand.'

'Oh, I understand only too well. I'm just sorry for poor old Ben. He never had much backbone.'

'He certainly didn't go through the fire unsinged,' said Oliver Fairleigh. He added, with a wicked anticipatory expression: 'However, I have made up for my bad behaviour. I have invited them to dinner next Saturday.'

'Saturday? But that's your birthday.'

'Precisely. I shall need the family gathering to be diluted. I shall need – how shall I put it? – diversionary targets.'

'Is everyone coming?'

'I believe so. Mark is apparently in the area – has even been home, though he made sure he didn't bump into *me*. No doubt I shall have news of his doings before long in the form of tradesmen's bills. Terence I gather has also signified that he will graciously take time off from making everybody's lives miserable with his cacophony –'

'It's quite a good group –'

Oliver Fairleigh indulged in a trumpet of elephantine disapproval. 'What nonsense! A good group! A contradiction in terms! People have gone mad! Someone will be recommending them for OBEs next!' He quietened down as the waiter poured him more wine. 'And then you'll be there, of course,' he went on.

'Oh yes, I'll be there.'

He gave her a look expressing the opinion that she would be the only thing that would save the day from disaster, and then they ate their meal in silence for a little. At last Bella said:

'Daddy –' (when she said that, with a wheedling upward

intonation, Oliver Fairleigh knew there was something special coming) 'why don't you surprise everybody this birthday dinner by being nice, the whole evening?'

The babyish expression appeared once more on her father's face.

'I tried it once. I got bored. Anyway, it made everybody twice as jumpy.'

'That's because you're usually only nice when you're planning something awful. I mean, be nice the whole evening, and the whole weekend, if necessary.'

'You can hardly expect me to be nice to Mark for one whole evening. Terence I might just manage it with, but Mark . . .'

'Yes, Mark as well. And Ben too – '

'And Ben's mousey little wife?'

'Does he have a wife?' Bella raised her eyebrows. 'Yes, of course. I'd forgotten. He's the sort that someone was bound to get hold of and cling on to, so that they both sink without trace together.' She remained a moment in thought, and then said: 'Yes, her as well. You like surprising people. Well, surprise them by being genial, and pleasant, and tolerant.'

'Tolerant!' snorted Oliver Fairleigh. 'The mediocrity's virtue!'

'Daddy!' said Bella. And then, with an implied threat in her voice: 'You do want me to come, don't you?'

Oliver Fairleigh looked pleadingly at his daughter, who did not soften her gaze. He returned to his plate, and toyed with his food for a little, but when he looked up again, the same stern gaze was upon him. At length he pushed his plate away.

'Perhaps,' he said. 'Let's talk about it.'

*Thursday*

Oliver Fairleigh's visit to London had gone very well. He had created hell at the BBC. He had delivered the last chapters of his new book to his publisher, and received the nervous homage due to a best-selling author. He had

partaken of a good meal with his favourite child. He had
heaved himself into his club in St James's, where old men
who had sodomized each other at school shook their heads
over the younger generation. All these things he had
enjoyed. It would be too much to say that they had put
him into a good mood, or made him at peace with the
world, but they had certainly made him feel that for the
moment life was bearable.

Eleanor Fairleigh-Stubbs was rather surprised. After the
euphoria had worn off, the period between books was
usually especially difficult. Yet here was Miss Cozzens
sitting in the study, putting her files in order and writing
replies to fan letters, and here was Oliver, walking with
her and Cuff in the gardens of Wycherley Court in the
early summer sun, for all the world as if he were an ordinary
country gentleman.

It wouldn't last. She had a sinking feeling in her stomach
that it wouldn't last into Saturday. Every year the birthday dinner – the preparations, the mere thought of it –
filled her with a gloom that was amply justified by the
occasion itself. It was the nadir of her year, worse even
than Christmas. But Lady Fairleigh was a hopeful
woman. If she had not been, she would not have married
Oliver Fairleigh. So she put her forebodings from her,
and tried to enjoy the brief period of peace.

'The roses are coming along well,' she said tentatively,
bending close and inspecting them for aphids with an
expert eye.

'Don't know how,' said Oliver Fairleigh, peering at
them less expertly, his gooseberry eyes popping out from
under flaring eyebrows. 'With that incompetent Wiggens
as gardener.'

'I see to the roses myself,' said Lady Fairleigh, with the
very slightest touch of asperity in her voice. 'As you know.'

'Probably accounts for it,' said Oliver Fairleigh. 'I
wouldn't trust Wiggens to water a pot-plant if I could get
anyone better, but I can't.'

'He does his best,' said his wife vaguely. 'Perhaps Bella

could find us someone – with her gardening contacts.'

'Bella doesn't know one end of a daffodil from the other,' said Oliver Fairleigh. 'And her only contacts would be with other young devils in a similar state of ignorance.'

'How did she look?'

'Beautiful as usual,' said Oliver Fairleigh, smiling benignly. He looked sunnily around the lawns and hedges and flower-beds that comprised his domain, and positively oozed self-satisfaction. 'We did a good job there, my dear,' he said.

Eleanor Fairleigh-Stubbs was rather surprised at the concession to her embodied in the "we". 'Such a *dangerous* name to choose,' she said. 'Lovely that it turned out right. Is she really liking the job?'

'Says she is.' Her husband's mood seemed to cloud over slightly. 'Just waiting to get on those damnfool colour supplements, I imagine. And sleeping around with that end in view.'

'Now *Oliver*, I'm sure you don't know she's been doing anything of the kind.'

'I've never known a girl that good-looking who wasn't sleeping around,' said Oliver Fairleigh, grandly general. 'That being so, I suppose she might as well do it with an end in view.' He added, as he so often did when talking about the affairs of his children: 'She can't expect anything more from me.'

Eleanor Fairleigh knew that if there was one person who could wheedle cash out of her husband, it was Bella, but she did not say so. 'She'll be coming to the birthday dinner anyway, won't she?' she asked.

'Oh yes, she's coming.'

'Perhaps we can talk about it then.'

'About what? Who she's sleeping with?'

'No – of course not. Just how she's doing, and so on – who her friends are. Girls will tell things to their mother that they wouldn't tell anyone else.'

It struck Oliver Fairleigh that his wife had a genius for

hitting on generalizations that were the exact opposite of the truth, but he was used to her combination of woolly thinking and unjustified optimism, and he seldom bit her head off more than three or four times a day, so he left her in her comfortable delusion.

'Well, I'm glad boys don't do the same to their fathers,' he grunted. 'I couldn't bear to be made the recipient of Mark's confessions.'

The name of that particular son was always a danger signal in conversations with Oliver Fairleigh. His wife, no wiser now than ever, weighed in with an appeal: 'But you will be nice to him on Saturday, won't you, Oliver?' As she said it, she felt sure she was only making things worse.

Oliver Fairleigh left an eloquent pause.

'Yes,' he said.

Eleanor Fairleigh was so surprised that she stopped in her tracks, and looked with earnest enquiry into her husband's face.

'What's the matter, woman? You asked me a question and I gave you an answer.' He continued on his way, with a sort of mock-aggrieved grumbling: 'It was a truthful answer, too. That's the trouble with women. They'll believe any amount of comfortable lies, but you tell them the truth and you haven't a hope of being believed.'

Lady Fairleigh-Stubbs put her arm through her husband's, and they continued their walk.

'Well, that *will* be nice,' she said. 'If you can. Because he's not a bad boy. And he's very good-natured.'

'He *is* a bad boy, and he is *not* good-natured,' said Oliver Fairleigh. He added, with a rare honesty: 'Not that I'd like him any better if he *was* good-natured.'

Eleanor Fairleigh was puzzled by his attitude. 'Just so long as you *try* to like him,' she said, smiling vaguely at a rhododendron bush and gripping his arm a little closer.

'I am most certainly *not* trying to like him,' said Oliver Fairleigh, irritated by the grip on his arm which seemed either proprietorial or conspiratorial. 'I said I would be nice to him on Saturday. That is the limit of my oath.'

'It's a start, anyway . . .'

'Sunday I do not vouch for. Sunday I said nothing to Bella about,' said Oliver Fairleigh with grim relish. Relieving himself of her arm he turned abruptly, and, kicking Cuff to follow him, stomped towards the house.

'Oh, Bella . . .' said his wife wistfully.

She turned and resumed her walk. The garden *was* looking lovely, though of course Oliver was the last person in the world to appreciate it. A garden to him was a sort of backdrop to his own performance; to her, since her children had grown up, it had become almost the most important thing in her life. She walked around, more briskly now that Oliver had gone, noting what was coming on well and what had not recovered from the drought last year. Finally she made for Wiggens, relaxing over his spade, and gave some directions about the flowers to be cut to decorate the house for Saturday.

'Family do, then, is it?' asked Wiggens, who had only been with them six months.

'Yes, Sir Oliver's birthday. All the family will be there – Bella, and Terence, and Mark.'

'Oh, Mr Mark too?' asked Wiggens, and it struck Lady Fairleigh that he gave her a rather odd look.

'Yes,' she said firmly. 'Mr Mark too.' And she turned and went towards the house.

When she walked into the kitchen, to see – in her vague way, for food did not interest her, except as a way of keeping her husband in equable mood – what was happening about lunch, she knew at first glance that Mrs Moxon had something to confide in her. Mrs Moxon was ample, reliable, and talented, and her only drawback was an insatiable curiosity and an unstoppable tongue. It was not just that one could not avoid hearing the affairs of everyone in Wycherley retailed at inordinate length; there was the question of what went in the other direction, from the manor to the rest of the village, and that worried Lady Fairleigh intensely. Not that it did her husband. He liked being talked about.

'I *was* sorry to hear about it, madam, I really was,' said Mrs Moxon, rubbing her doughy hands on her apron, and putting on an expression of sympathy profound enough for a family death.

'Sorry, Mrs Moxon? There's nothing to be sorry about. Nothing has happened.'

'Oh, then you've not heard about it, then, madam? Well, I'm sorry I mentioned it, I really am. Just that I thought you looked worried, so I supposed you must have heard.'

'Heard what, Mrs Moxon? Please don't be so mysterious. Come straight at it.'

'Well, it's Mr Mark, my lady. What he said at the Prince Albert in Hadley last Saturday.'

'He was drunk, was he?' said Lady Fairleigh-Stubbs, with a watery smile. 'Well, you've been with the family long enough to know that's nothing new, Mrs Moxon. And he *is* still young.'

'Oh, it's not that, ma'am. Of course I know all about that, and locking the spirits away, and all. Though never a word has crossed my lips, of course. But it's what he said – screamed through the whole pub, they say.'

'What did he say?' asked Eleanor Fairleigh, her heart thumping against her ribs.

'It was about his father,' said Mrs Moxon, now frankly enjoying herself. 'He said he ought to be shot. Straight out like that, shouted it through the whole pub. All the village is talking about it.'

Eleanor Fairleigh turned to go up the stairs. 'I expect it was just a joke,' she said. Even to herself she sounded feeble and defeated. She went up to her bedroom, and sitting wanly on the bed she found that her forebodings about Saturday had returned in full measure.

*Friday*
It was early evening, and Oliver Fairleigh had been sign-

ing letters – the grateful yet faintly magisterial letters that were sent in reply to his fan mail, and which were generally, in fact, the work of Miss Cozzens. The extent of his fan mail was always a matter of interest to Oliver Fairleigh, though he affected to despise the senders and made comments on their standards of literacy. Work on the last chapters of *Murder Upstairs and Downstairs* had meant that it had mounted up over the last few weeks, and signing the replies had put him in a good mood.

At present he was not alone in his study, but the interview he was conducting was not dissipating his good mood. Seen athwart the broad back of his interlocutor, his face glowed with lugubrious anticipation.

'I've no doubt I shan't like it,' he said with a genial snarl. 'Come along man, out with it.'

The broad back remained impassive, the large hands stayed respectfully at the sides, and the gentleman commenced a lengthy and circumstantial recital in a voice devoid of personality or drama. Oliver Fairleigh settled in his easy chair, and gave the narrative his attention only at those points that seemed important.

'Where?' he cut in. 'The Prince Albert? That mid-thirties monstrosity on the main road to Hadley – a pull-in for the middle-class motorist? I might have known he would drink at a place like that.' He grunted in contented gloom. 'Go on.'

His informant took some time to get into his stride again, but he regained Oliver Fairleigh's interest when he got to the conversation of the two couples in the pub.

'Talking about me, were they?' he said, as if the fact alone gave him pleasure, irrespective of what was said.

When the recital was finished, Oliver Fairleigh lit up a cigar, which only seemed to increase the geniality of his mood.

'Well, well,' he said, 'what a jolly little episode. I'm glad you picked it up, very glad. I'll be making it square with you.'

He waved his hand, which was rightly taken as a
gesture of dismissal. Left alone he remained pudgily sunk
in the easy chair, puffing contentedly. Twenty minutes
later, when the cigar was finished, he was still smiling,
though it was not a pleasant smile.


CHAPTER IV


OLIVER FAIRLEIGH'S SATURDAY


'THIS EGG,' roared Oliver Fairleigh, gazing bulbously
into its depths, 'has most certainly not been cooked for
five minutes.'

Sitting up in bed, a great Humpty-Dumpty figure, with
rolls of flesh pushing the buttons on his pyjama jacket to
bursting point, he looked like an eighteenth-century
princeling whose subjects are unreasonably demanding
bread. To Lady Fairleigh this, his morning look, was a
familiar sight, but not a particularly grateful one.

'Oh dear, hasn't it?' she said vaguely.

'Sack that woman.'

'Oh Oliver, don't be foolish. You know you could never
get anyone half as good. And as a matter of fact, Mrs
Moxon is busy preparing the birthday dinner. I cooked
your egg myself.' She looked distractedly at her wrist. 'My
watch is *very* small, and it's very difficult to see the
minutes.'

Oliver Fairleigh grunted. 'I'll go down and supervise
the meal when I've had breakfast,' he threatened.

'Oliver, please don't. You know she doesn't like being
watched. She's never yet let us down over the birthday
dinner. And I do think you ought to have the morning in
bed.'

'Why?' roared Oliver Fairleigh.

'Well, it is going to be a big day, and you know you're

not to overstrain yourself.'

'Rubbish,' yelled Oliver Fairleigh. Then, remembering, he reduced volume. 'Why should I overstrain myself? There won't be any scenes. I've told you I'm going to be good.'

'Oh Oliver,' sighed his wife. 'That of course will be the strain.'

Terence Fairleigh's room was at the back of the house, but it was a large well-proportioned bedroom with high ceilings, and there was ample room for amplifiers, loud-speakers, and the assorted junk of modern music-making. The walls were painted puce and green, both in shades of such virulence that his father had not entered the room since he first saw them. The decor was otherwise dominated by a large colour poster with the words *Witchetty Grub* in phosphorescent pink lettering across the top. It was the name of Terence Fairleigh's group. In the poster Terence (or Terry) was shown clutching a microphone as if it were the breathing tube on a crashing aeroplane. He was dressed in a skin-tight suit, every inch of which was spangled; the rest of the group were dressed, or in one case undressed, as the fancy took them.

Terence Fairleigh was not wearing spangles today. Even his mother would have drawn the line at that. He was wearing old jeans and a check shirt, and he was barefoot. His mother did rather dislike the bare feet, but she said nothing about them: today was Oliver's birthday, and she was again trying to look on the bright side and believe that for once, just once, the thing would go off without a hitch. What was more to the point than hazy optimism, she was doing all she could of a practical nature to ensure that Oliver's promise of good behaviour was not put to the test by any of the more predictable family phenomena that were the usual cause of thunderclouds.

'You will dress properly for dinner, won't you, dear?' she said, looking at her son anxiously.

'Of course, Mum. The whole hog, if necessary.'

'Well, it *is* the birthday dinner. I think your father would rather like it.'

'Then the whole hog it shall be,' said Terence, carelessly flipping through a magazine. 'And polite conversation throughout dinner – not a word of slang more recent than nineteen-twenty-five, not an obscenity, not a mention of music, and not a political opinion one centimetre to the left of Ghengis Khan.'

Terence looked at his mother, fair and open, his bright blue eyes utterly guileless.

'I know it will be a strain, dear. But it would mean such a lot to me to have a *happy* birthday for a change.'

'I doubt whether it will suit Dad. Why else have we kept up the custom but to have a satisfying occasion for fireworks in the middle of the year, to balance Christmas at the end? And of course it is *his* birthday. Still, I'll do what I can.'

'And then there's Mark – '

Terence held up his hand. 'Mum, I can exercise self-control, but I'm not a miracle-worker. Mark will have to take care of himself.'

'But that's what he never can do! If you could keep him away from the drink . . .'

'Mum, there's no way in the world of doing it. He's got a nose for it sharper than a beagle's, and ways of getting at it you and I couldn't begin to fathom. If you lock it away in this house, then he'll get it outside. Is he here yet?'

'No.'

'Then it's a near-certainty he'll arrive sloshed. The best thing you could do would be to put him to bed.'

'Oh, but I wouldn't want to do that. Your father promised to be nice to him – all day.'

'Christ! What's gotten into the old man?' As he looked at his mother enquiringly, his frank blue eyes took on an expression that was almost crudely speculative.

'He promised – he promised me – ' (a disinterested observer might almost have fancied that Lady Fairleigh-Stubbs was jealous of her daughter, so deliberate was her concealment here) – 'that he wouldn't let anything provoke him today.'

'Okay,' said Terence. 'Problem solved. So what are you worrying about?'

'Well, you can't always rely on your father's promises, you know. I think we should do our part too – not do things that we know annoy him. And if we *could* get the idea through to Mark – well, it might be a new beginning.'

Her voice had a vague wistfulness, as if even she could not believe such a thing possible. Terence smiled at her encouragingly. But as she left the room he lay back on the bed, stared at the ceiling, and furrowed his brow. Fancy his father promising good behaviour for one day. What was he up to? Or had the situation changed? Was this the result of some rapprochement between him and Mark? If so, what was Mark up to?

This needed watching, he said to himself, still gazing at the ceiling with his innocent blue eyes.

'Ben, do we have to go tonight?' asked his little wife in the kitchen of the little cottage without hollyhocks. 'It *is* really a family affair. We'll only be in the way.'

'We'll have to, Celia. He asked us specially, and there are not many people get asked there these days.'

'Not many who'd go, I shouldn't think,' said his wife.

'Of course he's a terrible old monster, I don't deny that. But he could be useful to me in a hundred ways.'

'Oh Ben, I realize that,' said Celia Woodstock. 'But the point is, *will* he? He hasn't exactly shown evidence of good will, has he? And I know I shall be so nervous, and frumpish, and clumsy – I'll annoy him every minute of the evening. I did last time, and I'm so nervous now it will be much worse tonight.'

'We don't have to stay long after dinner,' said Ben, wiping up a brown-veined plate that looked as if it might have been part of a large family service, but had seen better days. 'Then we can fade away. It's a long time since we saw the whole family together.'

'We?'

'Oh no, you don't really know them, do you? But it will be nice to see Bella and the boys again. Our families used to be quite close.'

'It's not a family I would want to be close to,' said his wife, quite waspishly.

'Wycherley double-two five one,' said Lady Fairleigh-Stubbs cautiously, in case it was someone to whom her husband had been rude. It was. 'Oh, Mark, lovely to hear your voice. Where are you? I wondered if you'd be here by now.'

Lady Fairleigh-Stubbs smoothed her hair as she listened for signs of slurring in her son's speech. At least he couldn't see her: he got so irate if he saw her listening for it, or thought she was trying to smell his breath.

'I see,' she said, when he got to the end of a story about having to meet a man about a deal, and their having missed one another, and having had to leave messages here and phone there. By now she was almost sure there was a slur, but she smiled brightly into the receiver. 'But you're on your way now, dear, aren't you? We'll expect you in an hour or so – ' And she put the receiver down on his plausible evasions.

'Still hoping for the best from Mark, Mother dear?' said a cool female voice, breaking into Eleanor Fairleigh's rather sad reverie like a March wind.

'Bella!' said her mother, and folded her in her arms. Bella was in travelling gear, but managed to show no signs of travel: how could anyone contrive to look like an ice lettuce on a hot summer's day, her mother wondered? Her make-up was bright and unsmudged, her blouse looked as if it were straight from the shop hanger, there was not a bulge in her slacks. It was almost inhuman. 'You look so lovely, my dear. I don't know how you manage it.'

'All for Papa's sake, of course,' said her daughter, with a slightly supercilious smile. 'Where is he, by the way? I'd better wish him happy birthday.'

'He's not down yet. He's been getting rather tired lately – what with finishing the new book, and the trip to London, and so on. I thought it would be best if he stayed in bed for a bit, and kept his strength up for the dinner.'

'All the better to give us hell with?' said Bella, resting her elegant case on the bottom stair.

'My dear, he's promised to be good the whole day – but of course, you know that: I gather it was your doing.'

Oh, so it was Bella's doing, thought Terence, who had been passing above on the landing on his way to the bathroom, but had stopped to listen in. Bella glanced carelessly at her mother, not quite sure of the meaning of the expression on her face.

'He's still going along with that, is he?' she asked. 'I'm flattered. Still, knowing Daddy's resolutions, he's not likely to keep it beyond the second sherry.'

'At least he's promised to make the effort,' said her mother, looking nervously upstairs in case he should descend in thunder, but seeing only the glint of light on her younger son's fair hair. 'It was really nice of you to persuade him.'

'I thought it would make a change,' said Bella, indifferently. 'And I felt sorry for Ben.'

'Ben Woodstock? Yes, poor boy. Your father was just a *tiny* bit difficult when we went round there. It will be pleasant having him tonight. It must be years and years since you saw him.'

'Oh, quite a time anyway,' said Bella, and not looking at her mother she swung herself and her suitcase upstairs to her bedroom.

'Everything seems to have blown over,' said Mrs Moxon somewhat regretfully in the kitchen, to Surtees, the chauffeur-cum-valet, who was tucking into a great meal at the kitchen table.

'Blown over?'

'That business of Master Mark – that scene he made at the Prince Albert.'

'Oh, that,' said Surtees, not letting such a triviality put him off his food. He was in his mid-thirties, stocky, and what Oliver Fairleigh would call vulgarly handsome – which meant that the observer had a suspicion he might use his looks to his own advantage. 'I reckon it's a bit late in the day to start taking notice of the things Master Mark says.'

'Sir Oliver likes a stick to beat him with,' said Mrs Moxon. 'But it seems to have been forgotten. Her Ladyship says she spoke to him on the phone, and he'll be here soon.'

'Let's hope he's sobered up, then,' said Surtees.

'How do you know he's been drinking?'

'I saw him at the Rose and Thistle, out Barclay way. And he'd had more than enough, I can tell you.'

'Oh dear,' said Mrs Moxon with relish. 'Poor Lady Fairleigh.'

Wycherley Court was an early eighteenth-century manor house, built by a gentleman who had done well out of the French wars. Like the great Marlborough (who had done even better) his instinct was to plant himself heavily on his native soil, as if daring God or the Supreme Being to uproot him. The manor he built was rectangular and solid, a matter of straight lines and angles at ninety degrees. When Oliver Fairleigh's rotund figure stood in the doorway, he looked like the circle in the square. Architecturally, the Brighton Pavilion would have suited him better.

It was five o'clock when Mark Fairleigh's Fiat drove through the gates and up the splendid circular drive to the front entrance. He was driving too fast, and his steering was too uncertain for comfort. The car skidded to a stop in front of the house, and there was an ominous pause before the driver got out. It seemed as though Mark was collecting his wits.

He got out of the car, and removed a small suitcase from the boot with a little too much care. His mother,

watching nervously from the hall, was glad to see that his
walk was steady enough: certainly he was not yet at the
staggering stage. But he tripped slightly on the top step,
and swore. By then his mother had opened the door to
him, and he looked hazily embarrassed.

'Mark!' said his mother, not embracing him because he
would suspect her of smelling his breath, but nevertheless
distinguishing on the breeze a mixture of gin and menthol
chewing-gum which she found unpleasant and ominous.
'You are looking well,' she said.

Mark certainly had a kind of bloom, though it was not
the bloom of health. His cheeks and temples were flushed,
and his eyes did not seem to focus properly: at the moment
they were straying around the large oak-panelled hall of
Wycherley Court, apparently looking for signs of his
father.

But Oliver Fairleigh was never just *there* – he always
appeared, always had to make an entrance. Today when
he strode in attended by Cuff, snuffling, there was a new
sort of effect. Today he was not Oliver Fairleigh, but Sir
Oliver Fairleigh-Stubbs: local landowner, adored squire,
a hunter and a fisher, a supporter of sound men and sound
measures, one of a class that has been the backbone of the
country from time immemorial. Odd that this im-
personation should have faint overtones that reminded one
of mine host at the local on Saturday night.

'Mark, my boy, good to see you!' he said, emerging
from his study in a lather of geniality, and baring his
teeth in a fearsome smile of welcome. 'Staying the night I
see! Keeping busy, eh? I'm glad you're here: I'd like
your opinion on a new consignment of port from Wither-
spoon's. Can't make up my mind about it – I'd like a
second view.'

If his father had put in his appearance in a scaly green
costume, breathing flames from his nostrils and dripping
blood from his claws Mark could not have been more
disconcerted. He backed two paces, swallowed, murmured
a vague assent, and then seemed inclined to turn to his

mother and ask what was up.

'Take your suitcase up, my boy, and have a bath if you want one. I'll have a sherry waiting for you in the lounge – or is it gin and tonic, eh? Haven't been keeping up with your tipples recently.'

Mark murmured that a gin and tonic would be fine, took up his suitcase again, and mounted the stairs – once more tripping on the top step, and swearing. He seemed to have a genius for not quite making it to the top.

'Well, well,' said Sir Oliver, not relaxing his mask even when alone with his wife, perhaps for fear it would crumble to nothing. 'Now we're all together! Nothing like it, eh, my dear? I have just a few more letters to sign – Miss Cozzens is really keeping me at it today – and then we'll all meet for a drink before dinner. Eh?'

And he pottered off – even his walk was different from his normal one – to his study, leaving his wife to gaze after him in bemusement. Oliver not flying into rages was one thing, Oliver positively genial was quite another. She had known it but once before: when he went to the Palace to collect his MBE, an honour which had pleased him out of all proportion to its worth. She did not know whether to find Oliver's behaviour today a pleasant change, or an alarming one. If only it had been she who had been able to persuade him into it, rather than her daughter . . .

Making up for the evening in her bedroom some half an hour later, and listening to the grunts from next door as her husband changed into his dinner-jacket, Eleanor Fairleigh-Stubbs looked at herself and wondered in her vague way why she bothered: why she bothered worrying, why she bothered trying to coax Oliver into good behaviour, why she bothered trying to build a normal family life. Oliver was Oliver; nothing would change him; he did not want a peaceful life, and those who were closest to him were too used to the scarifying changes of mood to value the brief cease-fires that were part of the household routine. It had never been a happy house, even when the children were young, even before the children had been born. She wondered why Terence and Mark continued to come home. Bella, of course, had a real affection for her father, or seemed to have, but the boys ... Why return to the battlefield if one didn't have to? Apart from to see her, of course. And because of the will.

She looked closely at her face. Forty-nine, and showing it: scrawny, worried, tired hair, unsightly throat. People said she was at a difficult age. All her ages had been difficult, and they had left their mark. The only thing to be said about her face, she thought, backing away from the mirror, was that it was undoubtedly aristocratic. It had style. It had breeding. Which is more than can be said for Oliver's, she thought grimly.

Oliver Fairleigh playing the country squire brought out the gentlewoman in his wife.

When she finally emerged from her bedroom, Eleanor met Mark on the landing and went down with him. He was trying to be bright, but not very coherently. He had not put on a dinner-jacket, and his mother suspected he had had more to drink. He had taken trouble with his tie, but it was somehow not quite square. The degree of concentration required to take one stair after another seemed that much greater than when he had arrived. Presumably the suitcase had contained a bottle. Eleanor Fairleigh-Stubbs smothered a sigh, and kept up light conversation. Mark replied, but too loudly.

Her husband was already in the lounge, and he welcomed them genially (again it was that landlord's heartiness, that grated on his wife) and sat them down. Mark tended to slump, and kept blinking his great, full, self-pitying eyes.

'Eleanor, my dear, a sherry for you? Mark – a gin and tonic?' He turned to the drinks cabinet. Eleanor noted that it was already unlocked – so as not to bring too obviously to Mark's notice the fact that because of him drink was always kept under lock and key in this house? How sensitive of Oliver, she thought, surrendering herself

to unrealism. Oliver brought the drinks over with a
paternal air.

'Well, Mark,' he said, sipping his own dry sherry, 'what
have you been doing with yourself?'

'I've been – I've been –' Mark took a gulp at his gin and
tonic – 'I've been making a lot of contacts.' He put his
glass down, carelessly, with a minor crash.

'Hope they're good ones. I remember when I was your
age – before your time, my dear – I was mad about
making contacts. People told me the literary world was an
in group, a clique, that I'd never get anywhere unless I
got myself in with them. What a lot of pushing and
shoving I went in for! I've never made such efforts! But
they paid off, too, some of those contacts.'

He sat back after this flow of reminiscence in pop-eyed
contemplation of his past, and let out a theatrical sigh of
satisfaction. Mark did not seem entirely to have been
following, but he said: 'You've got to have contacts.'

'One of them,' continued Sir Oliver, after giving his son
what was intended as a kindly look, 'was your cousin
Darcy, my dear –'

'Oh dear, Darcy –'

'Yes, well, perhaps not a happy topic of conversation,
but I met you at his place, you remember. And we were
engaged within the month. Ah, Terence – and Bella!'

Oliver Fairleigh's two younger children came in together, chattering happily. Both were impeccably, even
stylishly dressed, and Oliver Fairleigh could not forbear a
glance from Terence's dinner-jacket to the slightly
bedraggled lounge suit that his elder son was still wearing,
the appearance of which was not helped by Mark's
slumping posture in the easy chair. Terence was smart and
beautiful, with a classically regular face, distant blue eyes,
and long, fair hair, cut into a sort of halo round his face.
He was, Oliver Fairleigh thought, a suitable escort for
the aristocracy, and he was spending his time touring the
country with a band of raucous adolescents. At any other
time this thought might have prompted him to an

apoplectic outburst against his hair, or whatever grievance might be most conveniently to hand, but today, apparently, he was grateful for small mercies, and his surface geniality was undisturbed. He fussed over Bella and got her a drink, and the two younger children sat down on the sofa – elegant, slightly remote, handsome and well-heeled: they looked like a glossy advertisement: posed, almost too perfect.

'The Woodstocks will be here before long, I hope,' said Sir Oliver, settling back into his own chair and sipping his sherry again. 'You remember Ben Woodstock, Mark? You used to be great friends at one time.'

'Never liked him,' said Mark thickly.

'No, so often one doesn't,' said his father, popping his pudgy cheeks out. 'I hope you'll be nice to the little wife, my dear. She seemed to be a little lacking in confidence, poor child, and of course she doesn't know the young people, as Ben does.'

Eleanor bit back a reply to the effect that it was not she who was in the habit of intimidating the meek and mild, but she accepted, as always, the role allotted to her in the play Oliver was currently performing, and merely said: 'Yes – that's often very difficult when one is newly married.'

'I'll get the lad an introduction to Sir Edwin Macpherson, I think. I had a slight impression that might be why he invited us round last weekend. That should please him. Not that it will do any good, I'm afraid. No publisher is going to take on an author merely on my say-so. Still, the lad will have had his chance; and who knows, perhaps he has talent. Let's hope so.'

At that moment Surtees, who was butler for the evening, ushered in the Woodstocks, dressed in their best, which was somehow not good enough; they still seemed slightly moth-eaten, and destined for failure. As Sir Oliver overpowered them with genial hospitality, the little wife let out an audible sigh of relief.

Sir Oliver led them round, introducing Celia Woodstock to the younger members of his family. Mark was

blearily friendly in a way that suggested he would not
know who she was if he met her again tomorrow; Terence
was cool, Bella slightly distant: she cast her eye over the
large floral pattern on Celia Woodstock's dress, looked
directly into her face, smiled politely, then said no more.
Her father more than made up for it by seating her in the
best armchair, fussing over her drink, and engaging her in
conversation. Somewhat surprisingly, they found that
they had friends in common.

Within half an hour, Celia Woodstock was feeling
almost at home, and her only qualms occurred when she
caught sight of the elegant perfection of Bella, sitting on
the sofa with her husband, and talking – not about old
times, as one surely ought to on such occasions, but about
the world of publishing and journalism. They were very
animated. Ben's thin face was lit up, as she seldom had
seen it, and his hollow-chested body was alive with energy.
In the pause necessitated by Sir Oliver getting up to throw
a log on the (highly superfluous) fire, she noted Mark,
already on his third gin, and not focusing his eyes well:
she noted Terence and his mother, deep in a conversation
about dates and recording schedules, and she thought how
good-looking he was, but how – somehow – not really
*nice*.

Then Surtees came in, and announced dinner.

CHAPTER V

SUDDENLY AT HIS RESIDENCE

DINNER WAS GOOD. Dinner was Mrs Moxon at the peak of
her form. It would not have been like her to let any
inadequacies in her department disturb the equanimity of
Oliver Fairleigh on his birthday dinner, though she was

quite willing for it to be disturbed from any other quarter, being a woman who thrived on disorder. But when Surtees brought the plates down to the kitchen she was disappointed by his reports. There had been no explosion.

Everyone enjoyed the dinner, except Mark, who toyed nervously with it, downing a great deal of wine and seeming more interested in getting himself safely hoisted on to a cloud of oblivion than in anything going on around him.

Celia Woodstock put odious comparisons with her own performance firmly from her mind – after all, she thought, with the doggedness of the little woman, why *should* my dinners be compared with those of people who can afford to employ a cook? – and concentrated firmly on two things: her food and her host. She was seated beside Sir Oliver, and he was treating her with unending charm, asking her opinion on current events, showering her with anecdotes of the literary great, giving her fatherly advice, and even admiring her dress in a manner that seemed sincere. Celia Woodstock expanded into her dark green and orange patterned print frock, and came close to enjoying herself. It was not, unfortunately, possible entirely to relax: the dreadful shadow cast by Sir Oliver's performance last Sunday prevented her quite doing that. But she listened sensibly, she glowed now and then with pleasure, and she talked more than she usually did.

'Of course, I know people say that Ben is mad to think of becoming a writer full time,' she said confidingly. 'But he felt there was no job he could take that would leave him with the peace of mind to write, let alone the time.'

'A good point, that, very!' said Oliver Fairleigh, gazing at her with fatuous good-humour which a connoisseur of his performances might have caught as an imitation of a dim-witted Wodehousian club bore.

'After all, there are only two of us,' said Celia, looking at him appealingly, as if he were an old family friend to whom she had gone for advice. 'The cottage is ours, you know, and I'm perfectly capable of getting a job if necessary. Not – ' she lowered her voice – 'that it will be. As a matter of fact, we have a little more coming in than people imagine.'

Sir Oliver concealed a flinch at the vulgarity of the phrasing, and entered into the spirit of her confidences. 'I'm glad to hear it. Something tucked away, eh? A little nest egg? I wouldn't want to appear inquisitive, but I thought the family was – not to put too fine a point on it – broke.'

Celia Woodstock lowered her voice, dropped her eyes, and said: 'Not quite.'

'Good, good,' said Oliver Fairleigh, horribly avuncular. 'An independent income's the saving of a writer. Not a large one, necessarily, of course – '

'Oh, it's not large – ' said Celia hurriedly.

'But enough, eh? Well, I have a little surprise for you, my dear.' He patted her hand, and she looked down at his pudgy scrivener's paw in some consternation. 'I thought it might help if I introduced your husband to Sir Edwin Macpherson. Got the idea he wanted something of the kind, don't know why. So I thought I'd take him to lunch, some time in the next week or two – just the three of us.' Forestalling her little whinnies of pleasure, he directed his glance down the table. 'Ben, my boy – '

At the roar from his host Ben Woodstock looked up hastily and apprehensively from his low and intense conversation with Bella Fairleigh.

'I'm just telling your little wife, Ben, that I'm hoping to take you to lunch with Eddie Macpherson, if you could manage it. Do you think you could, eh?'

Ben Woodstock blushed pink, stuttered his thanks, and (as Sir Oliver turned his attention back to his food) looked enquiringly at his wife. Bella looked coldly in the same direction, but found Celia Woodstock gazing back at her, perfectly straight, with something close to a smile of triumph on her face.

'Of course,' said Sir Oliver, turning to her again, and

lowering his voice from a lordly bellow to a lordly whisper, 'beyond the lunch there's nothing much I can do. People think I can, but I can't. Can't force a man to publish a book if he doesn't want to. You're a sensible woman – you understand that. But we'll hope for the best.'

'This *is* kind,' said Celia sincerely. 'Ben is so pleased, I can see that. And his mother will be too.'

'Nice woman,' said Sir Oliver, licking his fat lips. 'Had a hard time of it. Sad to see the old families go down.'

'Oh, it is. The Woodstocks used to be the first family around here, so Ben says. Still, you never know: Ben always says the gentry have great staying power.'

'Does he?' said Oliver Fairleigh, gazing without any overt irony at Ben Woodstock's unimpressive form.

'I think over the years they've developed ways of holding on to what they've got,' said Celia Woodstock, conveying regretfully to her mouth the last of her boeuf bourguignon.

'Bella,' said her mother from across the table, anxious to disentangle her from the low, intense conversation with young Woodstock, which she could see was worrying his dull little wife: 'we were wondering if you could help us to get a new gardener.'

Bella raised her head and looked at her mother with something close to disdain. 'Mother dear, I suppose if you met Elizabeth David you'd ask her to find you a cook.'

'Well, I don't see why not – ' said Eleanor Fairleigh vaguely.

'I'm afraid that, though I'm working on a gardening newspaper, I have no contact whatever with gardeners. In fact, no one I meet has the slightest knowledge of gardening. We just put the paper together, and we hardly see the people who write it.'

'What a shame,' said her mother. 'So impersonal, somehow . . .'

'The best way to get a good gardener, mother, is to pay

well,' said Bella, and turned back to Ben Woodstock.
There was nothing for it for Eleanor but to talk to her
sons.

'Are you still thinking of moving, Mark?' she asked her
eldest.

'Sorry? . . .' Mark had been looking dully at his plate,
still well filled, and jiggling his glass to attract Surtees's
attention.

'Are you still thinking of moving, dear?'

'I've moved.'

'Already, dear? Where to? You will leave me your new
address before you go, won't you?'

'Islington,' said Mark, as if he hadn't quite heard. He
thought for a bit, looking drearily ahead, and then he
said: 'It's smaller. I didn't need all that space.'

'I'm sure it will be better, dear. After all, it will be less
to keep clean.'

Mark looked at his mother as if she were crazy, but was
diverted by the sight of Surtees with a full bottle in his
hand.

'Mark,' said Terence, from his mother's other side, 'is
not particularly interested in keeping his place clean. Nor
will I be when I have somewhere permanent of my own.
Cleanliness is very low on my list of priorities.'

'But you can't like living in *squalor*,' protested his
mother pleadingly.

'Of course he does,' came the genial roar from the head
of the table. Oliver Fairleigh was gazing in their direction
with an expression of fearsome good cheer on his face, like
a field-marshal visiting the Christmas Day dinner in the
NCOs' mess. 'Everyone should live in squalor when they're
young. Eh, Ben? I'm sure you did, before you did the
sensible thing and got yourself married.'

'Well,' said Ben weakly, 'I'm not a *tidy* person . . .'

'I should hope not. Filthy, I shouldn't wonder. That's
what makes people get married – being fed up with it.
Don't let your mother provide you with dusters and
vacuum cleaners, Mark, my boy. She cleaned me up, but

she shouldn't try it on you. Squalor is part of a writer's stock-in-trade.'

'I'm not a writer,' said Mark thickly.

'I know, my boy,' said his father equably. 'I was referring to myself. Though stranger things have happened, of course . . .'

'I'd rather die than be a writer,' went on Mark, oblivious of the pressure of his mother's hand on his right sleeve. 'Bloodless, sadistic bastards. Always taking people apart, pretending to understand – God, they're the last people to understand.' His great, dark-rimmed eyes watered with self-pity, and he looked with dull resentment at his father. 'Self-satisfied oafs,' he said. 'Think themselves bloody little gods. Playing with people . . . never leaving people alone . . . I'd rather die than be . . . than be a . . . writer.'

He subsided into a comatose silence, and looked at his untasted dessert. He had effectively doused the festive atmosphere. Oliver Fairleigh's eye glinted dangerously as he looked in his direction, and there was an edge to his voice as he tried – in a parody of the tactful host's manner – to fill in the surrounding silence.

'Of course he has a point,' he said generally, looking round the table. 'Wouldn't you agree, Woodstock? We are a pretty bloodless lot, I suppose – watching people, storing it all away. Eh? All the little details that fall into place later, all the little mannerisms that give people away. It must seem a pretty inhuman sort of existence, to people outside the charmed circle.' He lowered his voice, and addressed Celia Woodstock alone: 'He's had a little bit more than is good for him, you know. Not used to it.' And then, as conversation seemed to be slow in starting up around the rest of the table, he said: 'Shall we adjourn to the library? Surtees has put out the coffee there. I've one or two things I'd like to show your husband, my dear – he'll have to humour a bibliophile's whims for a little while, I'm afraid.'

They all got up, the Woodstocks saying all the right

things, and the little party trooped off towards the library. With one exception. As they reached the door they noticed that Mark had sunk back into his place, and his head was beginning to fall forward on to his chest.

Bella went back and leaned over him:

'Come on, Mark. Dinner's over. Come and have some coffee. That'll buck you up.'

There were clotted mutterings from Mark that sounded like obscenities. Bella started to lift him.

'Leave him, Bella,' said her father, his voice dangerously close to a shout. 'Best to let him come to on his own.'

'Oh no, Daddy. This is the best part of the dinner. Mark will have to be in on it.' And Bella and Terence between them stood Mark up, and – staggering slightly, for Mark was not a small man – they hoisted him across the hall and into the library. Once they had him there they let him sink into an easy chair by the door, where he promptly went to sleep, if he had ever wakened.

The study was large, luxurious and dark, lined with cupboards and bookcases, whose contents were predominantly brown and nineteenth-century-looking, though there were two shelves over the desk which contained a long line of books in gaudier dust-jackets, no doubt the host's own collected works. The desk itself was an enormous, heavy Victorian affair, and was open.

'My goodness!' said Oliver Fairleigh, looking at it. 'This is a surprise!'

It was piled high with presents, large and small, all wrapped in luxurious sorts of wrapping paper.

'My husband is a terrible child,' whispered Eleanor Fairleigh to Celia Woodstock. 'He loves presents. We put them here every year, and he always pretends to be surprised.'

Oliver Fairleigh had capered over to the presents, and was rummaging around in the pile with little porcine snuffles of glee. ' "From Bella, with love"! Goodness me! It's quite heavy. What can it be? From Terence, this one: what a nice *big* parcel. It can't be handkerchiefs, that's a blessing. Leave handkerchiefs for people who like picking their noses. This is Eleanor's – it rattles. What can *that* be? Cuff-links, perhaps? Not a lighter, anyway. I'm not supposed to smoke, Celia, my dear – ' he drew Mrs Woodstock into the family group by the hand – 'and my wife would regard a lighter as an encouragement. And here's one from Miss Cozzens. How very friendly. Perhaps I should have invited her to be with us tonight. Do you think it was remiss of me, Eleanor, my dear? Will she hold it against me?'

Oliver Fairleigh's voice trailed away, as he finished inspecting the pile of presents. There was an awkwardness as everyone realized that there seemed to be one lacking. Oliver Fairleigh looked towards Mark. He said nothing. Then, rubbing his hands, he flashed his teeth into a rather frightening smile – Celia Woodstock remembered last Sunday, and shivered suddenly – and said:

'Now, Eleanor, if you'll be so good as to see to the coffee, I'll pour the liqueurs.'

'Oh, Oliver, should you? Why don't you open your presents first?'

Oliver Fairleigh looked longingly at the decanters along the shelf of the open cupboard behind the desk, and longingly at the presents in their gaudy pile. The presents won.

'Well, well,' he said; 'perhaps if I just took a peep . . .'

The world is divided into those who eat their meat first, and those who eat their vegetables. Oliver Fairleigh was decidedly of the former type. Ignoring Miss Cozzens's small, square box, he dived for Bella's present, and handled it lovingly: a substantial, heavy and interesting parcel. His podgy fingers struggled with the wrapping, and when he had got it off he dived down to look at the contents, screening them from the gaze of the little knot of people round him. Little snorts of delight and appreciation were heard, and ecstatic shakings of the shoulders.

'Look!' he said. 'Look!' The others regarded this as licence to swoop down around him, only Bella standing a little aloof, smiling to herself. '*Caleb Williams,*' said Oliver Fairleigh. 'The first edition. What a find!' He straightened and turned to Celia Woodstock. 'It's the first detective story, you know, or more or less. Bella, my dear, you are a dreadful daughter. You must have spent three months' salary. I have an awful presentiment that I shall be forced to subsidize my own birthday present.'

He kissed her heartily, and she put her arms elegantly around his thick, publican's neck.

'You're very unfair, Daddy. I haven't asked you for a penny since I started work.'

'That,' said Oliver Fairleigh, who never lost his realism in money matters, 'is because you know how to work me up to offering it you whenever you find you need it.'

Terence's present was a substantial and handsome silk dressing-gown, beamingly received. Eleanor's was indeed cuff-links, traditional and solid, and she was given a husbandly kiss of thanks. Miss Cozzens's was handker-chiefs.

'Oh, how fortunate I *didn't* ask her tonight,' said Sir Oliver. 'It would have been very embarrassing. What could I have said? You know, one of her great advantages as a secretary is that she has no imagination, so it would be very ungrateful of me to complain.'

By now the group around the desk had dispersed around the room, and Sir Oliver surveyed them all with a cheek-popping beam on his face.

'A wonderful birthday,' he said genially. 'The best for years. So kind of you, Celia and Ben, to come and share it with us.' He turned and took a cigar from a box on top of the desk, ignoring an inarticulate protest from his wife. 'Tomorrow we must go out somewhere – for a meal, or a drink. I feel the need to spend something on my family, after all their generosity.' He lit his cigar, and puffed away at it appreciatively. 'Where shall we go? I hear the Prince Albert at Hadley is one of the places people go these days.'

There was a sudden silence in the study. Eleanor's

heart seemed suddenly to suspend operations. Oliver Fairleigh was looking genially in the direction of his elder son, but if he hoped for a reaction, he was disappointed. Mark, deep in sleep and deep in his chair, gave little sign of life beyond the slight regular rise and fall of his chest. For a few seconds the host of the evening savoured the silence in the room, savoured the infinitesimal look of enquiry that passed from his daughter Bella to his son Terence, noticed that the embarrassment of the Woodstocks made it perfectly clear that the village gossip had got to them. Then he rubbed his hands and turned back to the desk.

'Now, Eleanor, perhaps you will pour the coffee. If it's cold you must blame me. Liqueurs, everybody?'

From the low cupboard just above the desk Oliver Fairleigh took a series of decanters and bottles.

'I love liqueurs,' he said happily to Celia Woodstock, as if in an attempt to restore the happy atmosphere. 'It's deplorable, but I'm afraid I have to admit to a sweet tooth. What will you have, my dear? Cointreau? Grenadine? Or what about my own special favourite – it's called lakka. You won't have heard of it. It's Finnish, and it's made from cloudberries – quite delicious.'

He took the stopper from a decanter with a small quantity of yellow liqueur in it.

'It's awfully sweet, disgustingly sweet,' said Eleanor. 'You might not like it. We have to get it specially from the Finnish Tourist place. I'm sure no one else in Britain drinks it.'

'I think you may be right,' chortled Oliver Fairleigh happily. 'Except expatriate Finns with sweet tooths, or should that be sweet teeth?' Everyone smiled nervously. It was now clear to all, even the non-family members, that it would not do to be too sure of their man. 'Now, my dear?' he enquired, smiling ingratiatingly at Celia Woodstock.

'I think I would prefer cointreau,' she said, in the nervous voice of one who knows nothing about liqueurs, and does not expect to like them.

'Very well, cointreau it shall be; and the same for Eleanor – ' Oliver Fairleigh poured a succession of little glasses and handed them round. By now they had all managed to seat themselves around the heavy, glowering study, except for Ben Woodstock, who had been drawn to the bookshelves – or perhaps who had felt he ought to show an interest in his host's collection. After handing a glass of drambuie to Terence, Oliver Fairleigh looked at his elder son, still comatose in his armchair at the far end of the room.

'We'll leave him, for a little,' he said, as if Mark were an underdone roast, and turned back to pour himself a little glass of thick yellow liqueur from a rather fine cut-glass decanter.

'Now,' he said – but before he could propose a toast, his wife and daughter both said, 'Happy birthday, Oliver!' and they all raised their glasses, or in some cases their coffee cups, to him. With a contented expression on his face, relishing, as always, being the centre of attention, Oliver Fairleigh drank his lakka. He drew together his formidable eyebrows. He pushed his tongue experimentally through his lips. He let out a grunt – expostulatory, bass, frightening, but finishing in an odd, questioning little whimper. He fell heavily to the floor.

'Oliver! My God! I knew this would happen.' His wife had jumped from her chair, upsetting the table beside it and the coffee cup on it. She dashed over to the bulbous, collapsed figure by the desk. 'Surtees! Someone get Surtees! Ring for an ambulance, quickly!'

She was hardly on her knees beside her husband when Surtees dashed into the room.

'What is it? I was passing – ' He saw Lady Fairleigh on the floor, and ran over to where she was, finally seeing the body, moaning and feebly thrashing around. 'Water. Get some water.' He threw some flowers from a vase on a side-table to the floor, spread the body of Oliver Fairleigh out lengthways, and dashed the water into his face.

'For heaven's sake, man, it's not a faint or a fit,' said Lady Fairleigh. 'Get him up. He's supposed to sit up.'

'This is Wycherley Court,' said Terence in an unnaturally high voice into the phone. 'Will you send an ambulance at once. It's my father – Sir Oliver Fairleigh-Stubbs. Quickly, please. He's had some sort of attack.' He pressed down the receiver rest, and immediately began dialling again.

'He doesn't seem able to breathe,' said Eleanor Fairleigh. 'What should we do?' She looked at Surtees, who was trying to prop up the immense bulk of his employer in a sitting position, and was sweating with the effort. 'Perhaps we should lay him down after all,' his wife said. 'I'm sure he would be more comfortable. Do you think we should try massaging his heart?'

'Dr Leighton? It's Terence Fairleigh. Dad has had an attack – heart, I think. Can you come? ... Yes, he is, but he's in a bad way. I've called for the ambulance ... Yes, please hurry.'

Terence Fairleigh put down the phone. 'He'll be here right away,' he said. 'He said that was what he was afraid of.'

He looked at the three figures on the floor, and then turned round to look at his sister. She was standing a few feet from her father, seeming as usual to carry a quality of remoteness with her, but her eyes were awash with tears, and her mouth was twitching.

'Mummy,' she said. 'I'll go with him in the ambulance. You'll only upset yourself.'

Eleanor Fairleigh straightened her back. 'Indeed you will not, Bella,' she said directly and determinedly, looking unblinkingly at her daughter. Then she turned back to her husband.

Terence put out his hand and took Bella's in his.

Half an hour later the ambulance had been and gone, conveying swiftly and efficiently Sir Oliver and Lady Fairleigh. Dr Leighton had driven up as it was leaving, and had relieved Surtees of the task of going with them. The Woodstocks had taken the opportunity to slip off, after a few words of sympathy and hope to the ones left behind.

'I'm sure he'll be all right,' said Celia Woodstock to Bella, her face assuming a standard expression.

'Oh? Why?' said Bella. Her eyes were quite dry now, and they looked directly at Celia. She turned away, discomforted, and she and Ben were soon seen walking down the drive, he long and cadaverous, she short and homely. From a distance they seemed oddly ill-assorted. They were not talking.

At ten forty-five the phone rang. Terence Fairleigh was there in a second, and snatched it up.

'Wycherley two-two-five-one. Oh Mother ... My God – so soon? ... I felt sure it was going to be all right. I didn't expect ... Shall we come? ... Dr Leighton? All right, I'll tell Surtees to make you something. Goodbye, Mum.'

He put down the telephone. 'He's dead,' he said. He looked at Bella, whose eyes once more were overflowing. 'Mum's coming back now with Dr Leighton.'

Bella seemed about to sink down into a chair and crumple up. Terence took her hands, held them tight.

'Don't break down, old girl,' he said. 'Think of Mum. We two'll be all right.' But when she looked at him there was distrust in her face.

They were disturbed by a noise from near the door. Mark, deep in his armchair, first grunted, then rubbed his hands in his eyes, and then opened them, looking ahead blearily and uncertainly.

'What time is it?' he said. 'Why are you still up?'

He saw the decanters in the open cupboard, and focusing his eyes on them he began to struggle to his feet.

'Arise, Sir Mark,' said Terence contemptuously.

### CHAPTER VI

## Mourned by his Family . . .

Barbara cozzens really rather enjoyed the morning after her employer's death. She was a tower of strength in a crisis, she felt – without, naturally, pushing herself forward or intruding where she was unwelcome. Her unflappability and her excellence at coping were qualities which had not been called on the previous evening: indeed, if she had not slipped down to the kitchen after she heard the ambulance drive away, she might not have known that her employer was even ill. Once down there, she had allowed Mrs Moxon to administer coffee, and they had stayed on chatting in whispers (though why in whispers in that enormous kitchen with no one remotely near to overhear them she would have been at a loss to explain). Surtees, with their encouragement, went back-wards and forwards periodically to the study, ostensibly to clear away the coffee cups and glasses. When he brought the news of Oliver Fairleigh's death, the two ladies had both said 'No!' Then they had all switched to brandy and begun to discuss their futures.

This morning she sat at the desk where Sir Oliver only a few hours before had opened presents and dispensed liqueurs, dealing with enquiries and setting in train arrangements for the funeral. The death had been too late for the Sunday papers, but had been broadcast on the eight o'clock news. The secretary of the Crime Writers' Association phoned her official sympathy, as did some fellow detective writers: there was little grief, but much tact. She spoke to Gerald Simmington, Sir Oliver's editor at Macpherson's and (circling round the subject in the manner of those who are being worldly at a time when

they feel they ought to be spiritual) they agreed how
fortunate it was that *Murder Upstairs and Downstairs* had
been finished before the tragedy of the night before.

'Because I certainly didn't know the solution myself,'
Miss Cozzens confided. 'And the public wouldn't have
been very interested in an unfinished detective story,
would they? After all, it's not as though he was Dickens . . .'

As Miss Cozzens sat at the desk, conspicuously coping,
her thoughts turned to her own future. They were helped
in this direction by Cuff, who sat at her feet, but kept
making sorties round the room, whining wheezily and
looking bewildered. Cuff knew things were different, and
Miss Cozzens faced up to the changes in her own life too.
Perhaps she regretted them less than Cuff did. Of course,
first she would have to stay on for a few weeks here,
perhaps a few months, for she knew more about Sir
Oliver's literary and business affairs than anyone in the
house and she would be needed – or 'indispensable' as she
put it to herself. After that – a holiday, a late holiday, a
real Indian Summer, in Greece, or Southern Italy, or
perhaps the West Indies. Then a new job. It would have
been nice to have a change from authors, she thought
wistfully, but it seemed foolhardy to waste her experience
of the last few years: having worked for Oliver Fairleigh,
she could pick and choose in the literary world. And after
all, she could not be sure that a businessman or a politician
would turn out any better.

She would be careful what *kind* of writer she engaged
herself to, of course: nothing would induce her to consider
employment with a romantic lady novelist, for example:
candy-coated sarcasms and slavery for a pittance were the
fate of those who let themselves fall into that trap. But a
biographer would be nice, a sort of popular historian. Her
capacity for research had never been properly exploited in
her present job, especially as Sir Oliver had been so
criminally careless over details. The sort of person who
wrote biographies of the Romantic poets or the Queens of

England would suit her down to the ground, thought Miss Cozzens, warming her feet on Cuff.

She was in the middle of constructing this particular aerial edifice when she was interrupted by the ringing of the telephone. She set her face in an expression of containable grief, and took up the receiver:

'Oh, Dr Leighton, how good of you to ring . . . No, Lady Fairleigh is already up, and taking it very well, considering . . . It's not as though it's entirely unexpected, is it? I believe they're in the sitting-room now – I'm trying to keep all the worrisome stuff from them, till they're more used to the idea, more able to cope . . . I'm sorry, Dr Leighton, could you repeat that, I don't quite understand . . . Not satisfied? But . . . an autopsy . . . *police*, but . . . Are you sure you wouldn't like to tell Lady Fairleigh about this yourself, Dr Leighton? . . . Of course, if you wish it, I'll tell her . . . Thank you Doctor, it's kind of you to say so . . . I'll tell her straight away.'

But when she put down the phone, she sat for some time, staring ahead of her, her face still wearing the mask of decorous grief, but her forehead slightly creased. Then she got up, squared her shoulders, and walked resolutely to the door.

'Of course, one keeps *saying* it's not unexpected,' said Eleanor Fairleigh, putting down a cup of strong coffee, and looking round at her children; 'I'm sure Miss Cozzens is saying that to everyone at the moment. But when it comes to the point, it *isn't* expected, and the shock is just as great, however many doctors' warnings there may have been.'

'Still, it's not as though Father was an easy person to keep in order,' said Terence, his voice on a very even keel. 'Doctors' warnings didn't mean much to him.'

'Well, but he did try, you know,' said his widow. 'He very seldom smoked, and he had cut down on his drinking an awful lot. He never took spirits at all, and only the occasional glass of lakka at weekends. Really, you know, considering your father's character, he was surprisingly good.'

'But there was the wine,' said Bella. 'Daddy said he'd rather die than give that up.'

It wasn't a fortunate expression. Bella was looking less than her perfectly groomed self, though still enormously self-controlled. Her hair was falling around her shoulders with hardly a wave, and some of her make-up looked left-over from last night.

'In any case,' said Mark, sober and suited, though somewhat bloodshot of eye, 'he kept the keys, so he could always have helped himself whenever he wanted one.'

'But I kept a very good eye on him, you know, dear,' said his mother. 'And so did Miss Cozzens. Of course there were occasions when he had one or two when he shouldn't: like finishing the last book, for example. But on the whole I think he stuck to the routine Dr Leighton prescribed, with his own little modifications. I must say I was astonished at how well he kept to it. I think in his own way he enjoyed life.'

'I'm sure he did,' said Mark inscrutably.

'Doesn't anyone feel like a drink now?' said Bella. Her mother shot her a furious glance, and attempted the hopeless task of shaking her head imperceptibly. Bella ignored her. 'Well, I do, anyway,' she said, marched to the cupboard and took out a bottle. She poured herself a neat whisky. 'No one else?'

'No thanks, Bella,' said Mark, drinking the last of his coffee and setting his cup down.

'No thanks,' said Terence after a pause.

Bella had effectively destroyed the atmosphere of discreet family mourning. They all sat there, trying not to look at Mark, wondering at his refusal, and wondering what to talk about. Eleanor felt a wave of relief wash over her, dousing the anger towards her daughter. She thanked heavens there had not been time to try and stop Mark from accepting, otherwise she surely would have driven him to doing it. The others juggled feverishly with possible topics of conversation. Money, of course, was out. It had to be something with reference to Father, but without reference to his will. It was not easy.

'I hope his last book is good,' said Bella at last, perhaps feeling a mite repentant. 'It will be so much better to go out with a bang, and so much more like him.'

As if on cue, Miss Cozzens came in with the bang.

'Lady Fairleigh, I wonder if I might talk to you for a moment,' she said.

'But is it anything the children can't hear, Barbara?'

'Well, no, I suppose they'll have to know. But it's a little difficult to explain. Dr Leighton has just rung – '

'So kind. He has been *very* good all the time.'

' – and he says they're not completely satisfied at the hospital about the cause of death.'

'The cause of death, Barbara? But it was a heart attack. I told them about Oliver's heart.'

'They're not quite satisfied about the cause of the attack, he says. They're not quite sure that it was caused naturally.' Miss Cozzens was so embarrassed that she could hardly look at them straight as she said it.

Eleanor Fairleigh-Stubbs looked at her in increasing bewilderment, and then looked round at her children. '*Naturally*. But how can a heart attack be natural? I don't understand what – '

'Mother,' said Bella in a flat, brutal voice, 'did you never read any of Daddy's books? They think someone killed him.'

'Bella!' Her mother's mouth gaped, her eyes filled with tears, and she seemed to crumple up.

'Now please, Lady Fairleigh, nothing whatsoever has been said about any such thing,' said Barbara Cozzens briskly. 'There is merely a question of an autopsy, to determine the cause of death with complete certainty. I'm sure we're all much too sensible to jump to conclusions, aren't we?' She threw a disapproving glance in Bella's direction, but Bella continued sipping her whisky and staring straight ahead. Miss Cozzens thought to herself that she seemed to have lost a lot of that quality of coolness which had always been her great weapon.

'Miss Cozzens is right, Mother,' said Mark. 'I'm sure it's just routine. It will all be cleared up in a few hours.'

'And if it's not?' said Terence significantly.

'Terence!' said Barbara Cozzens sharply, addressing him for the first time for some years by his Christian name. 'I should have thought you'd have had more sense – '

'If it's not,' said Mark, not avoiding his gaze, 'we in this family ought to know what follows.'

Eleanor Fairleigh, who had been gazing wide-eyed at all her children, at last broke down into sobs. Her tall, strong-boned body heaved up and down, and sounds came from her that were at once heartbroken and terrified. Mark went over to her chair and sat down on the arm. 'Now, come on, Mum,' he said, putting his arm around her. 'They're just being silly. You know how we are sometimes. There's no question of anyone having killed him. Just bear up. You've had all the strain. Come on, Mum, don't break down now.'

'Really,' said Miss Cozzens (the approaching termination of whose employment seemed to have loosened her tongue), 'you two should be soundly spanked.'

'For facing facts?' said Bella. She looked challengingly at Barbara Cozzens, and then beyond her to the door. Surtees was standing there, and behind him, keeping in the shadow, was a man in uniform. They were obviously considering how to break in on the scene, and Bella wondered how long they had been there.

'Excuse me, my lady,' said Surtees, 'but this is Chief Inspector Meredith.' He seemed to want to say more, but couldn't get it out, so he retreated into the murk of the hall, where other uniformed figures seemed to be waiting.

'I'm sorry to have to trouble you, Lady Fairleigh,' said the Chief Inspector, his mouth set in an expression of grief, but his eyes dancing and sparkling as if they belonged to another play, 'but it's perhaps best to talk to you all together.'

Miss Cozzens's heart gave a strange leap, as if she had been here before. For the voice, pleasant and musical, had an unmistakable Welsh lilt.

CHAPTER VII

SAID THE PIGGY: I WILL

INSPECTOR MEREDITH was a chunky man of middle-height, who could once have been a rugby scrum-half, but had not acquired the bruiser's face that sometimes goes with the game. He was in his early forties, his hair still light brown untouched by grey, his face mobile and candid, and his eyes dancing with pleasure and mischief and joy in life. Whatever effects a policeman's lot had on other members of the force, it did not seem to have robbed Inspector Meredith of a boyish zest for experience. Even when the rest of his face was trying on other expressions for size, his eyes said he was enjoying himself hugely, rippling like a lake in a spring breeze. At the moment he looked more as if he had just solved a difficult case instead of being just about to begin one.

The eyes, darting lithely, took in Bella and Terence, both apparently relaxed in their chairs, but looking at him tensely; took in Mark, indefinably crumpled, but managing a certain dignity as he sat comforting his mother; took in Miss Cozzens and the odd mixture of respectability, disapproval, efficiency and covert enjoyment somehow mingled in her face and stance; took in Lady Fairleigh-Stubbs, struggling to wipe away the tears from her long, mobile, distinguished face. It was she in the end who reacted to his arrival. She dabbed determinedly at her face, assumed with an effort a brave front, got to her feet and advanced towards him, hand outstretched. It seemed like a heroic triumph of breeding over inclination.

'Good morning, Inspector,' she said, shaking him by the hand. 'I'm afraid we are a little upset here, as you can imagine. Perhaps you had better sit down.'

'Thank you, Lady Fairleigh.' Chief Inspector Meredith, his face set more than ever in a mask of sobriety, darted over to a chair, sat himself neatly in it, and looked around once more at the family of Oliver Fairleigh. Mark was standing now, and trying to coax his mother back to her seat. Bella and Terence had not acknowledged his presence – had, in fact, hardly moved a muscle, except to turn their heads slightly so as to follow him with their eyes. A very chilly pair indeed, Meredith decided.

'You won't thank me for beating about the bush, I'm sure of that,' he said, putting his open palms squarely on his knees. 'I'm here because we're afraid that your husband's heart attack, ma'am, was in some way or other induced. Of course we are not sure of anything yet, but we suspect that it may have been brought on by some poison that acts on the heart – nicotine, for example.'

'Nicotine?' said Lady Fairleigh, who for all her efforts still seemed to be in a state of shell-shock. 'Well, of course, Oliver had lit up a cigar.'

'It would have to be nicotine administered in some other way, say in a liquid solution,' explained Meredith patiently. 'Of course, whether this was taken accidentally, or deliberately, or was administered to him by another person we have no means of knowing as yet. That's what we are here for.'

'You mean,' said Mark, 'that his death was either suicide, or accident, or murder.'

'That's correct, sir.'

Meredith looked round at the five faces, all trying to digest the implications of what he had just said.

'I'm sure there's no question of suicide,' said Lady Fairleigh at last, apparently with reluctance. 'As we were just saying, Oliver loved life, in his own way.'

'How could a poison like that get into anything

accidentally?' asked Miss Cozzens. 'It doesn't seem possible. Especially as only Sir Oliver was affected.'

'It is rather difficult to imagine,' said Inspector Meredith. He paused, and let the third alternative hang for a moment in the room, like a bat in the rafters.

Half an hour later the sequence of events on the previous evening was becoming a little plainer to Meredith.

'So if we assume – a big assumption, I'm perfectly aware – if we assume that the cause of death was the lakka, then it seems to me that the likeliest thing is that the poison was introduced into the glass. Otherwise any number of people could have been poisoned.' The Fairleigh family considered this thoughtfully. 'And the glasses – ?' continued Meredith.

'They've been washed up, Inspector,' said Barbara Cozzens, feeling less than usually irreproachable at the thought that it was she who had encouraged Surtees to be so officiously efficient the night before. The Inspector looked at her, but if he was annoyed he didn't let it show on his face. His habitual airy good-humour was undisturbed.

'Ah well, that's a pity. Never mind. My men can get the glasses that were used. There's no telling what tiny traces may still be clinging to them.'

'But you know, Inspector,' said Terence, who had dropped his passive hostility, 'I don't remember too clearly – we'd all had quite a lot to drink at dinner – but I *think* Dad poured out his lakka and took it up in his hand immediately. Then we toasted him, and he drank it down. Isn't that right?' He looked round enquiringly at his mother and sister.

'Yes, it is, dear, I remember it distinctly,' said his mother. 'He drank it almost immediately. So you see, it's quite impossible, Inspector.' She said it with an eager satisfaction, as if having proved this one hypothesis to be impossible, the whole nightmare would go away. Inspector Meredith felt that she was not doing justice to her intelligence.

'Was there an interval between his pouring the glass before his own and his pouring his own?' asked Meredith. 'If there was, the – poison might have been introduced into the glass before the liqueur was poured into it.'

They all furrowed their brows. 'I think there may have been,' said Bella finally. 'Was it your glass he poured before his own, Terry?'

Terence shrugged. 'Search me. It's not the kind of thing you would remember, is it?'

'I think it was,' said Eleanor Fairleigh, 'But I couldn't be sure.'

'In any case,' said Meredith, 'we'll soon know, because my boys will be examining the decanter of lakka.'

'If the poison – if there *was* poison – was put in the decanter, there wouldn't have been any great risk,' said Terence. 'None of us would have touched the stuff. Only Dad drank it.'

'But you had guests,' said Meredith.

'Of course,' said Terence carelessly. 'I'd forgotten the Woodstocks. They are rather the sort of people one tends to overlook.'

Meredith noted a glance pass from Bella to Terence, of what meaning he could not guess. Lady Eleanor was thoughtfully continuing on the same track: 'Of course, I remember now, Oliver did press little Mrs Woodstock to try the lakka. How lucky she refused.'

'And of course,' said Meredith, 'if the poison was put into the decanter, it could have been put there at any time since the last occasion anybody drank the stuff. So whoever it was did it may not have known that there would be guests to dinner next time it was used. Or of course,' Meredith added, 'he may not have cared.'

'The cupboard where the decanter was was always kept locked,' said Miss Cozzens. 'And Sir Oliver kept the key himself. Whoever it was would have had to break into the cupboard.'

'Oh, he always kept the keys, did he? Why was that?'

'One of his little ways,' said his widow hurriedly. She

did not look at her children. Meredith sat in thought for a few seconds.

'Let's forget that possibility for a moment,' he said at last. 'Now, while the presents were being opened, you were all crowding round the desk – is that right?'

'Except Mark,' said Eleanor, quickly again.

'Oh yes? And why was that, sir?'

'I was drunk,' said Mark, without embarrassment. 'You'll have to ask the others what I did. I don't remember anything after dinner. When I woke I was in the chair by the door, that I do recall. But by then he was dead.' Mark looked round, wide-eyed and enquiring at his brother and sister. Inspector Meredith sensed in them a certain reluctance to offer testimony on this point. Terence looked as if his thoughts were elsewhere, while Bella looked at her glass.

'We brought Mark from the dinner table to the study,' said Bella at last. 'Terence and I. We put him in the chair.'

'Did he leave it at all during the festivities?'

'I don't think so.'

'Bella, you know perfectly well he didn't,' said her mother, her voice rising.

'I didn't *see* him leave it,' said Bella, with an edge to her voice too. 'I wasn't paying any attention to him. Why should I? I was looking at Daddy and the presents.'

'He didn't get up,' said Eleanor, in a forceful, landed-gentry voice. 'I was watching him.'

'The whole time?' said Meredith suavely, not taking his eyes off her. 'Why was that?'

'Because he was drunk. Any mother would be worried.'

'I see.' It occurred to Eleanor in a flash that the Inspector knew that her son was an habitual drinker. It occurred to her too that he had heard of the incident at the Prince Albert at Hadley. She groaned inwardly. But then, he was bound to hear before long. If the servants didn't tell him, Terence or Bella would.

'Well,' said Meredith, getting up, 'I must go and see how my men are doing, and ring the hospital. I think that will be all for the moment, but I presume you will all be staying in the house?' He looked, raising his eloquent eyebrows, particularly at the three children of Oliver Fairleigh. They all nodded. 'That's all right, then. Because I shall probably need to see you later in the day.'

'If they do find poison,' said Eleanor, shakily defiant.

'If, as you say, my lady, they do find poison.'

'Excuse me, Lady Fairleigh,' said the voice of Surtees from the doorway. 'Mr Widdicomb is here.'

The family exchanged glances, then, conscious of Meredith's eyes on them, wished they had kept them to themselves.

'Will you show him in, Surtees?' said Eleanor Fairleigh.

Mr Widdicomb, it was clear to Meredith at first glance, could only be a lawyer. Meagre of form, pin-striped as if by nature, his face cautious, unemotional, non-committal. He looked like a dyspeptic bird with whom life had not on the whole agreed. He acknowledged Meredith's presence without surprise: clearly Surtees had told him of the state of affairs, or else he had heard of it before setting out, by some mysterious lawyer's channel.

'Perhaps I could see you afterwards?' murmured Meredith at the door. Mr Widdicomb assented by a sharp little bow of the head, and Meredith slipped out of the room.

All Mr Widdicomb's movements were precise and unobtrusive: he advanced towards the family group in a manner almost mechanical. 'A sad occasion, Lady Fairleigh,' he said, in a voice devoid of all passion and grief, high and desiccated. 'We shall all be the poorer for his going.'

This last remark – so patently untrue as far as the dead man's family were concerned – caused a smile of cool amusement to waft briefly over the face of Terence Fairleigh. The phrase was one Mr Widdicomb was accustomed to use of dead clergymen and other putatively indigent worthies, and his use of it now suggested that the news of the police investigation had marginally upset him, for it was very unlike him to put a foot wrong on these occasions. He compressed his lips, and looked with some annoyance at Terence Fairleigh. Lady Eleanor acknowledged his professional sympathy by a droop of the eyes, and gestured him to a seat.

'Thank you, thank you.' He perched rather than sat, clutching his briefcase to his abdomen and darting looks around him with bright, unsympathetic eyes. 'I need not say I am anxious to spare you all the worry I possibly can, Lady Fairleigh. Though as far as the police are concerned, there are, of course, limits to what one can accomplish.'

'I'm sure they will realize their mistake very quickly,' said Eleanor. 'It will all be cleared up in no time.'

'No doubt, no doubt,' said Mr Widdicomb, not bothering to put any conviction into his voice. In his experience the police did not begin investigations into cases of suspected murder without being fairly sure of their ground first.

'If you'll excuse me, Lady Fairleigh,' said Miss Cozzens, glancing tactfully towards the door.

'Oh yes, Barbara, of course,' said Lady Fairleigh distractedly. Mr Widdicomb's stainless-steel eyes registered her going and the punctilious closing of the door. Miss Cozzens was a type of which Mr Widdicomb, in his bloodless way, approved.

'Ah yes, now, as I was saying, should you need me in the next few days, regard me as absolutely at your disposal. Absolutely. The police can be unduly high-handed in such matters, though I intend no judgement on the Inspector in question, who is unknown to me. But it is as well to be prepared – upset as you already are.' He looked around him, as if to assure himself that they were upset to just the decorous degree, then opened his briefcase and began taking papers out of it. Mark quietly got up and moved a side-table to beside his chair. 'Ah, thank you, Sir Mark,' said Mr Widdicomb.

Unnoticed by him, or at least not obviously noticed by him, a glance passed between Terence and Bella at the bestowal of the title, a glance not of the most pleasant.

'Now,' said Mr Widdicomb, placing his briefcase meticulously down by the chair and laying out the abstracted papers on the side-table, 'I take it that in general terms you are all familiar with the contents of Sir Oliver's will?'

'No,' said Terence.

'My husband usually kept such things to himself,' said his mother. 'It was not the sort of thing that he felt should be discussed in the family.'

'Ah? Is that so?' said Mr Widdicomb. 'Well, well, it's a perfectly straightforward document, perfectly straightforward. Drawn up by himself, I may say. He merely sent it to me to remove ambiguities and suchlike. I mention this because the phraseology is hardly as I would have liked it myself. I have noticed that in his charming books Sir Oliver was – however, *de mortuis*, eh? Let me see, the will is dated September 10th, 1976 – nine months ago, in fact.'

'Nine months?' said Bella.

'Yes. Now, there are some preliminary small bequests. Two hundred and fifty pounds to Barbara Cozzens, I quote, "my secretary of several years' standing, to compensate her for the exquisite and prolonged boredom of transcribing my literary works." Very charasteristic touch that! Delightful sense of humour!'

Mr Widdicomb glanced over his spectacles at Oliver Fairleigh's family, and decided they did not show the same appreciation of the dead man's humour as he professed himself. He blinked, and dropped his eyes back to the will.

' "To John Surtees, the sum of five hundred pounds, for faithful service" – very generous and proper. Sir Oliver if I may say so was a man who always knew the right thing to do.' Mr Widdicomb appended to himself the addendum 'even if he did not always do it,' for he had been the victim of several bouts of Oliver Fairleigh's persecution over the years. 'Now, "To my dear wife Eleanor, who has her own sufficient income, I bequeath all my personal chattels, and the copyright of my novel *Black Widow* for her lifetime, in testimony of my gratitude for nearly thirty years of devoted companionship." ' Mr Widdicomb bobbed his head in Lady Fairleigh's direction: 'Most moving.'

'It was what I expected,' said Eleanor, looking round at the children. 'Of course, I have more than enough for my own needs. Oh dear, *Black Widow*. I don't remember it at all. I suppose that's Oliver's sense of humour again.'

' "To my dear son Terence I bequeath absolutely the copyright of my novel *Foul Play At The Crossroads*, to be of support to him when his musical activities should cease to entertain the British public." '

A shadow flitted across the handsome face of Terence, and he shifted position in his chair so as to be able to see Bella on the sofa.

' "To my beloved daughter Bella, I bequeath the copyright of my novel *Right Royal Murder*, not my best but my most popular work, as testimony to my great love of her, and in order to keep her over the years in the little luxuries to which I imagine she will not become the less addicted." '

As Mr Widdicomb's voice faded, Bella sat tense, as if waiting for more. 'But – ' she said, flushing.

' "I devise and bequeath all the residue of my real and personal estate, whether of property, shares, money or copyright in my other works, to my son Mark, to be his absolutely, in the confident hope that he will be worthy of the family name." Dear me, not well put, not well put at all.'

But it was not the phraseology that was affecting his hearers. Terence's gaze, and that of Bella, had now shifted, and they were both gazing incredulously at Mark. Mr Widdicomb foresaw the sort of scene that he made it his business if possible to avoid. He shuffled together the papers and reached down for his briefcase.

'There are a few more remarks of no great importance that I need not trouble you with now. Needless to say, you will all be sent copies of the document. If I may say so, a most proper disposition of his property, most proper – hmm, granted, as I say, some oddities in the wording.'

He rose to his feet, and walked over to Mark, with his hand outstretched.

'Is that will legal?' broke in the harsh voice of Bella. 'Is it properly witnessed?'

Mr Widdicomb, caught with his hand outstretched in something approaching a ridiculous position, turned towards her with the nearest thing to asperity he permitted himself with the family of a client. 'My dear young lady, you could hardly imagine that I would take the trouble to read to you from an unwitnessed document.' His voice positively crackled with disapproval. 'The will is perfectly legal.'

Bella sustained his look for a second, then the corners of her mouth seemed to crease down with disappointment. 'That,' she said bitterly, 'was Daddy's last surprise ending.'

Mr Widdicomb pursed his lips, turned away from her, and fulfilled his intention of shaking hands with Sir Mark. His natural inclination to keep in well with the man in possession tied in on this occasion with his sense that Mark was the only one of the children who had behaved properly: that is, he had held his tongue. Mr Widdicomb had heard rumours on the subject of Mark Fairleigh – had, indeed, heard his father expatiate on the subject at considerable length one day in his office – but he owned himself agreeably surprised by his conduct on this occasion. He turned to take the hand of Lady Fairleigh, dropped a few words of arid comfort on her head, nodded to the youngest children, and made for the door. Mark ushered him out, and the two exchanged some words, apparently arrangements for some future meeting.

Bella continued to sit rigid, staring straight ahead of her: her mouth had stopped working, and was now set in a straight line. Terence, on the other hand, seemed to be taking longer to gain control over himself. His eyes were round and liquid – they were, in fact, oddly reminiscent of the old Mark. Eleanor Fairleigh remained in her chair, looking at the hearth-rug. The news had not elated her. She could only think to herself: what are the police going to say about this?

Mark closed the door authoritatively. Walking back to the little group, a disinterested observer would have sized him up as a presentable, well-brought-up young man who had gone through a difficult time: his manner was good, his bearing and expression public-school, but not offensively so. The whole set of his body seemed to say that at the moment they might all be going through a tough time, but that he was now in charge, and would see them through it all right. His gaze, though still slightly bloodshot, was perfectly serene.

'Nearly lunch-time,' he said quietly. 'I'm sure you could do with a sherry, Mother. I should think we all could. Is it dry for you, Bella?'

And he walked confidently over to the drinks cabinet.

'God damn you to hell, Mark!' shouted Bella, her face crimson with fury as she flung herself from the room.

CHAPTER VIII

STRONG POISON

'It seems,' said Inspector Meredith, 'a perfectly straightforward division of the property.'

Mr Widdicomb shut the will away in his briefcase hurriedly, as if it were a rare item of Victorian pornography which he had been allowing Meredith to cast a glance over, and said: 'Quite.'

'The books, the ones left to the mother and the younger children, they will bring in a fair amount of money, I presume.'

'I imagine so,' said Mr Widdicomb, gazing around the oak, book-lined study as if it were witness enough to Oliver Fairleigh's prosperity. 'You would have to consult Sir Oliver's accountant for details, but I assume it will bring them in a little nest egg every quarter or half year.'

'The books seem popular.'

'Yes, most of them seem to be kept in print. One sees them – on railway bookstalls, and suchlike places.'

'You don't enjoy them yourself?'

'I imagine that no one who had any professional acquaintance with crime or criminals would be likely to find them very convincing.' Mr Widdicomb's expression was of the most dyspeptic, and Meredith had the impression not only that he had found his late client profoundly distasteful, but that on the present occasion he was holding back a strong inclination to say something sharp about the same gentleman's family.

'Of course,' said Meredith, at a hazard, 'younger children these days always have the idea that they should be treated on an equality with the eldest.'

'They do. Frequently,' said Mr Widdicomb, with icy warmth. 'It is not an idea with much to be said in its favour, in my opinion. Our old families have enough to contend with as it is, without that.'

'You think in this case the younger children expected more?' asked Meredith, rather disappointed by Mr Widdicomb's cautious habit of speaking in generalities.

'That I think you should ask them,' said the lawyer, rising and smoothing down the jacket of his suit. 'You must remember that the family are my clients.'

'Of course, of course. I suppose you would not wish to tell me whether you yourself were surprised at Sir Oliver's disposition of his property?'

'I presume you are alluding to the relations between him and his eldest son?'

'Precisely.'

'It is not my job to be surprised. I merely had the will made out in my office. Sir Oliver's opinions on the subject of his son were no business of mine. He did not see fit to discuss the main provisions of the will with me, nor did I expect him to.'

'But you did have direct dealings with him over the will?'

'Certainly. He signed it in my office, where it was witnessed by two of my staff. It was, in fact, substantially the same as Sir Oliver's previous will: the provisions for Miss Cozzens and Surtees were new, and the book whose copyright was given to Bella was changed – that, as I remember, was all.'

'Why was the book changed?'

'I imagine it was a more popular title than the previous choice. *Right Royal Murder* came out last year, you remember, in good time for the Queen's Jubilee. A catchpenny idea, if you want my opinion, and quite unworthy of an author of Oliver Fairleigh's standing, but the book proved very successful. No doubt that was the reason for the change. Now, if you will allow me, Inspector – '

And Mr Widdicomb made for the door.

Mr Widdicomb, thought Idwal Meredith to himself, tried to have it both ways: to be at once an oyster of the old school and to make sure that his opinions – especially his disapprovals – were known and felt. Meredith had the impression that should the need absolutely arise he could get quite a lot out of Mr Widdicomb.

Meanwhile, what he needed was someone more obviously loose-tongued, to fill him in on the sort of family background that the family themselves were unlikely to be forthcoming about. He had rather liked the look of Surtees when he had shown him in – or rather, he had liked the look of him as a potential witness. He looked at his watch. Probably he would be still occupied with lunch. On an impulse he took up the phone and dialled headquarters.

'Any results yet? . . . Oh, just come in . . . I see. The decanter and one of the glasses . . . Interesting . . . A solution – strong enough to kill a normal man? . . . I see – and with his heart condition that made it quite certain . . .

Good. Keep at it, and I'll chug along at this end.'

He put down the receiver, fireworks of anticipation in his eyes. Now he had a case. Now everything could be open and direct, without the 'ifs' and 'on the other hands.' Nicotine poison. An unusual method, but easy enough to obtain, if you knew the way. It always terrified Meredith, in fact, to think how very easy poison was to obtain, if you knew the way. Luckily very few people did, or there would probably be far more murders which were cheerfully accepted as death from natural causes.

Meredith slipped out into the hall, and stopped to speak to Sergeant Trapp, massive and rural, who was stationed there to co-ordinate the work of the detective-constables in the various parts of the house. Trapp was being watched beadily by Cuff, who seemed to regard sergeants as a sadly deteriorated race of men.

'We have a case, Jim. It was nicotine in the decanter. I want your boys to get hold of the clothes everyone wore that night, and put the forensic chappies on to them. Oh, and you'd better send over and get them from the Woodstocks too, and all the servants. Anyone who would have had a chance to go into the study that night.'

'Big job, sir.'

'What are the labs for, if it's not for jobs like that?' Idwal Meredith's voice had the slightest note of contempt in it. As he spoke he saw Surtees emerge from the dining-room with a tray full of dessert plates in his hands. He put the tray on to a side-table, and closed the door quietly. Then he went through into the servants' quarters.

'Tell me, Jim,' said Meredith softly, 'what's your opinion of that gentleman?'

Sergeant Trapp surreptitiously drew his hand from behind his back, and with his fingers and thumb illustrated the notion of a duck, quacking.

'That was rather my impression,' said Meredith. 'I think Surtees is my man at the moment.'

Lunch was not an easy meal for any of the three who took

it. Mark and his mother tried to keep the conversation on neutral topics, but after a death and a will, there suddenly seemed to be no neutral topics left in the world. They discussed the funeral, but could come to no firm decisions in view of the uncertainties caused by the police. They broached the possibility of a memorial service, but (without their saying so) it occurred to both of them that it would turn into a gathering of people Oliver Fairleigh had insulted, congratulating themselves on having the last laugh.

Mark drank, with lunch, one and a half glasses of white wine – less, in fact, than Terence. There was a palpable effort involved, but he won a clear victory over his inclinations, and by the end of the meal seemed to be in a mood of some serenity. His mother felt that, on this score at least, her heart should have been light, but in fact her feelings were mixed: what would the police think about a young man whose alibi for his father's death was that he was drunk, who was – to all appearances – a confirmed alcoholic, yet who underwent a miraculous cure the moment his father died? Over and over Eleanor Fairleigh found her mind returning to the question: what will the police think? Which was odd, for she had so far admitted to no one that her husband's death could conceivably be a case of murder.

Terence's mind was on other things. He sat slumped through the meal, hardly bothering even to toy with his food, the picture of romantic melancholy. When he spoke it turned out that (like so many romantics) he had been thinking of himself and money.

'*Foul Play At The Crossroads,*' he said abruptly, 'which one is that?'

'It's about witchcraft,' said Mark. 'I remember it coming out, because the money paid for my twenty-first party. It was very popular – witchcraft always goes down well.'

'Yes, it's odd, isn't it?' said Eleanor brightly. 'Witchcraft and royalty, they're always popular. Whereas some

of the ones that Oliver really liked himself never caught on
in the same way. I'm sure he thought a great deal before
he chose those two for you and Bella, Terence. He was
very fond of you both.'

Terence's mouth curled unpleasantly. 'That's all very
moving,' he said. 'There's a lump in my throat. But the
fact is, we get one each. Mark gets – what will it be? –
about twenty-eight.'

'Thirty-two,' said Mark quietly.

'Thirty-two. Always in print, sold at every damn book-
stall you go to.' He looked at his brother with a look of
sheer malevolence: 'I shall choke every time I see them.'

'Terence!' said his mother.

Terence brooded further through the sweet, and then,
over coffee, said: 'Did you know he'd left you everything?'

'No,' said Mark. 'He never discussed the will with me.'
Then, after a pause, and apparently impelled by a desire
to be completely honest, he said: 'I suspected it.'

'Why?' asked Terence. And then again, louder: 'Why?
He hated your guts.'

'Apparently,' said Mark, with some dignity. He sat for
some moments in thought, as if trying to decide whether to
say something. He seemed to decide not to, but he turned
to Terence with a brotherly smile, as if he was anxious to
put relations between them on a casually friendly footing,
though the expression on his brother's face did not suggest
he would succeed easily. 'He may have hated my guts, but
I think in some ways I understood him better than you or
Bella. Of course, if he'd wanted to show how much he
loathed me, he could very easily have cut me out of the
will. Or he needn't have gone that far: he could have left
you and Bella a lot more of the copyrights to his books.'

'Well, why didn't he?'

'Because he wanted to keep this place going, keep it
intact from father to son – he wanted to establish us as the
squires of the place. You know he had this image of himself as squire of Wycherley. He'd been playing the part for
so long, off and on, that it had become part of him. He

knew whoever inherited would need as much money as he could lay hands on to keep the place going, and since I would inherit the title, it had to be me. I had to have the rest as well. That's what I think you and Bella never realized.'

'Such a ridiculous title,' murmured Eleanor. 'So ludicrous of Oliver to pay so much attention to it.' She looked dismayed at her youngest son, still sitting slouched over his coffee-cup with the expression of a petulant gigolo. 'I'm sure Mark is right, though. Your father wanted to keep everything together. It wasn't that he loved you and Bella any the less.'

'I don't care a fuck whether he loved me or not,' said Terence. 'I expected more.'

'I don't think Father would ever have cut me off, however he felt about me,' said Mark, still admirably cool and collected. 'Unless I had been involved in something really disgraceful, something criminal.' He gave his brother a long, meaningful look. 'Perhaps in your heart of hearts you did realize that, Terence.'

For a second, Terence's mouth dropped open, like a schoolboy caught out in a lie. He squirmed in his chair, and seemed about to run from the room. To fill in the awkwardness, his mother said: 'And, of course, now Mark is head of the family, he'll naturally feel an obligation towards you and Bella, if you should get into difficulties or want to branch out in any way. I'm sure he'll always be only too glad to help you.'

'Of course,' said Mark. 'Within reason.'

Later, walking in the garden, and watching Wiggens weeding the herbaceous border with highly unsteady hand (he had been selling the inside story of the Wycherley Court murder to a succession of customers at the local who were sceptical of his information but willing to pay for the privilege of being the first to hear it), Lady Fairleigh-Stubbs meditated on the new Mark: there was an almost frightening sudden maturity about him, a sense of responsibility, a calm capability that was both astonishing and welcome. There was also, it seemed to her, a cool calculation that lay quite outside her previous experience of Mark. She found it, she decided, disconcerting – almost frightening. By what quirk of genetics, she wondered, had the children of Oliver Fairleigh all turned out to be such cool customers?

Surtees was far from unwilling to talk. He was so willing, in fact, that he was reluctant to share Meredith with Mrs Moxon, and took him into the room off the kitchen which had once served as the butler's pantry, and was now apparently his own private nook. It was an untidy, unprepossessing room, with odd heaps of newspapers and weekly grub-sheets scattered around, a portable television in the corner, and photographs sellotaped to the wall – some of relatives and old girl-friends, Meredith conjectured, and some soft porn pin-ups, glossy, explicit and anonymous.

'We'll be more cosy-like in here,' said Surtees ingratiatingly, ushering him in, and throwing a threatening look behind him to Mrs Moxon, as a warning against listening in.

Meredith had not found his first impressions of Surtees very favourable. Certainly he was good-looking, in a fleshy, heavy sort of a way. His profile was classical without being in the least refined, his body capable, even powerful. The man, Meredith thought, for a g.b.h. charge, rather than a poisoner. There was too about him an air of self-satisfaction and self-seeking, as if he would do almost anything in the moral calendar if the price was right – and shop his customer to the authorities afterwards, if it suited his book. If he had been a policeman, he would probably have been in the vice squad.

'I suppose you want to hear about last night?' asked Surtees, 'all the details, and what everybody did, eh?'

'That first of all,' said Meredith.

'Well, of course, I didn't see it all, because I was in and out the whole time. But I'll tell you what I did see.'

Meredith found Surtees's narration absorbing. As far as reporting what he saw went, Surtees seemed an excellent witness. There were, Meredith thought, three salient points in his description of the previous night's birthday dinner. The first was that Oliver Fairleigh had been in an extremely, in fact an incredibly, genial mood all evening, that he had paid particular attention to Mrs Woodstock – 'Normally she was the sort he kicked as he passed, and then went back to do it again,' said Surtees – and that he had not allowed his mood to be upset by any of the things that as a rule could unfailingly have been relied on to produce thunder from the deep.

'Why do you think that was?' asked Meredith.

'Search me. According to Mrs Moxon, he'd promised Bella to be nice as pie to everyone the whole day. She may be right, but she gets things arse-up fifty per cent of the time, silly old moo.' He brought out the shop-worn phrase as if it were a new-coining of his own, smiled a greasy smile and then drew his hand across his mouth in a man-among-men gesture.

The second salient point was the behaviour of Bella Fairleigh. Surtees was in no doubt whatsoever that she had been making a dead set at Ben Woodstock from the moment he arrived.

'Can you be quite sure of that? After all, beyond talking, they can't have *done* very much at the dinner table.'

'I know the signs, believe you me, Inspector. There are ways of talking, and ways of listening too. That dreary little bundle his wife saw it too, and has probably made the house too hot to hold him today, I tell you, there's no mistaking things with our Bella: if she has her eyes on someone, they show the scorch-marks pretty fast. Not that I can see what she sees in him. Straggly bit of nothing, I'd have said.' And John Surtees looked down at the fleshy bicep straining against his rolled-up shirt, and made no attempt to hide his complacency.

'When you say you know the signs,' said Meredith,

himself now putting on his most deceptive air of man-to-man confidentiality, like two Welshmen Sunday-drinking, 'do you mean she'd tried out her techniques on you, eh?'

Surtees smiled his oily smile. 'Come off it, Inspector,' he said. 'I'm not the sort to kiss and tell.'

Though that, Inspector Meredith thought, is precisely the sort that you are.

The third point of interest was the condition and behaviour of Mark Fairleigh. Meredith had already learnt that he had been drunk; now he heard that he had abused his father at table. It was, Surtees asserted, very much Mark's normal way of behaving whenever he came home, though on this occasion his father had restrained himself from replying in kind.

'Restrained himself,' said Surtees, 'with difficulty. No doubt saving himself up for later.'

'Are you quite sure,' asked Meredith, 'that Mark Fairleigh was drunk? And not just pretending?'

'Sure as I'm sitting here, I know the signs,' said Surtees, once again using the phrase that seemed to sum up his pride in his worldly knowledge.

'He seems a sober enough type today.'

'Shock,' said Surtees. 'It takes some people that way. It won't last, I'll tell you that.' A smirk of anticipation spread over his face: 'Got another shock coming to him, I shouldn't wonder, that'll knock him straight back off the wagon, you see if it doesn't!'

'What's that?'

'The will. He won't be getting much out of his old dad, that's for sure. No one would blame him either, the things that boy has done over the years.'

'What sort of things?'

'Oh debts, scrapes with the police, drunk and disorderly in every pub in the area practically. Only last weekend he was broadcasting to all and sundry out at the Prince Albert, Hadley way, that his father ought to be shot.'

'Do you think his father heard about it?'

'He heard.'

'But of course they've probably learnt what's in the will already.'

' 'Course they haven't. They have to have the reading after the funeral, don't they? All sit around the table and pretend they don't care one way or the other, then the lawyer reads it out and an almighty row blows up. That's what'll happen. Seen it lots of times on the telly. We do things right in this house.'

Meredith was rather pleased to find that he was right to limit Surtees's reliability to what he had seen with his own eyes. Outside it he seemed to conform to the usual mixture of credulity and salacious speculation. Meredith merely said: 'If he hasn't left it to Mark, who do you think he will have left it to?'

'Oh, stands to reason, the lot to Bella. Something nice to little Mr Snake-in-the-Grass Terence, a tie-pin or a pair of old socks to Mr Mark, and the rest to Bella. I bet little Terry has a shrewd idea that's how it will go too. He's been like a bear with a sore head all through lunch.'

'Well,' said Meredith, once more with his secret-beer-drinkers air, 'I suppose you'd know. He confided in you, didn't he?'

'Old Lord Almighty? Confide in me? Not him. All get and no give, as far as information was concerned. No, as I say, it stands to reason: she was the apple of his eye. Made sure she was too. "Daddy this" and "Daddy that" the whole time.'

'She sucked up to him, did she?'

'Not exactly that. Not in any obvious way, anyway. She just kept him interested, kept him watching her: it was more like a boy-friend she wanted to keep on the boil if you ask me. But she had him in the palm of her hand, where the others bored him stiff.'

'You said he liked getting information. What did you mean? Information about Mark, for instance?'

'Oh yes, him and anyone else. He liked to know things.

He was a conner-sewer of human nature, you might say. But particularly Mr Mark – yes, he liked to know what he was up to.'

'Did you give him information yourself?'

'If I got any. Why not? I don't owe that little sot any loyalty that I know of. I'd be out on my ear if he had anything to do with it – not that he will.' Surtees's expression was unpleasantly anticipatory, as if he foresaw for himself a special position in a Wycherley Court owned and run by Bella Fairleigh.

'What did you do last night after you served dinner? Was it you or Sir Oliver opened the cupboard with the liqueurs in?'

'Me. Why? Was it the liqueurs did for him?'

'Possibly.'

'Thought so, when I saw his glass on the floor. So someone got at the lakka, did they? Yes, it was me. After I'd served the sweets, I came down to the kitchen and hurried up old mother Moxon with the coffee. Then I took it up to the study, and opened the drinks cupboard at the same time.'

'Did you have a key to it as well?'

'Not on your life. See Sir Oliver trusting anyone else with one. No, he gave me his just before dinner, as per usual.'

'How long was the cupboard open before they came into the study from dinner?'

Surtees shrugged his heavy shoulders. 'Matter of two or three minutes, no more than that. I went into the dining-room after I'd put the coffee in the study. Mr Mark was having his little outburst about how he would rather die than be an author. Silly little shit, what does he know? Anyway, that put the damper on things, so pretty soon they went over to the study – Miss Bella and Terence dragging Mark.'

'So none of the family could have got at the lakka between your opening the cupboard and the whole party going across to the study for coffee?'

'Not a chance, mate. They were all at the table the whole time.'

'Who got to the study first – was anyone ahead of the others?'

'Sir Oliver went in first, with Mrs Woodstock, but he wasn't far ahead of the others.'

'Do you think any of the family could have had a duplicate key to the cupboard?'

Surtees thought hard. 'No, I don't. The locks on the drinks cupboards both in the study and the lounge were changed a couple of years ago, when little Lord Fauntleroy was going through a bad period – correction, when little Lord Fauntleroy was going through a *particularly* bad period, because he hasn't had a good one since he was nineteen or twenty, so far as I've heard. Anyway, Sir Oliver had the locks changed, making it a good excuse for not even giving me one of my own, and he never let those keys out of his sight, except now and again to give them to me on nights when there were guests.'

'And you – ?'

'If you mean, did I get duplicates made for anyone, you can stuff the idea, matey,' said Surtees, taking advantage of Meredith's matiness because it pleased him to be able to give the police a bit of cheek. 'I'm the great incorruptible, that's what I am. Or shall we say my loyalty was to Sir Oliver, no one else. It doesn't do to sell your soul too often. Especially not when Sir Oliver had such a very good information service.'

Meredith rose to go. 'It's been very interesting,' he said. 'Just keep your eyes open in the next few days, will you?'

'Sure thing,' said Surtees ingratiatingly. 'Better not ask what it's worth to you, had I? You cops can turn funny about little things like that. Still, if I'm ever in trouble in the future, I can just quote your name, can't I?'

'Of course, of course,' said Meredith at the door, mentally adding: 'You can try.'

Back in the study Meredith tried to sort out his impressions. He had already had, before he came, a mental picture of Oliver Fairleigh, culled from local gossip. His morning in Wycherley Court had not radically altered that impression: the man seemed to have been an unpredictable and erratic tyrant, ruling a disunited and unsatisfactory family. Beyond the family circle, Meredith had no reason to doubt that Oliver Fairleigh was a man with so many enemies that a list of people who might have *vaguely* wanted him out of the way could easily run to three figures. Yet the man must have been more complex than this outline. There was, for instance, the will, the strange decision to leave everything – virtually – to a son he hated.

Inspector Meredith idly went over to the shelf behind the desk at which Oliver Fairleigh had drunk his last toast. Here were ranged, he had already noted, the English first editions of Oliver Fairleigh's works. He took out *Foul Play At The Crossroads*: a photographic cover, sky blue, depicting a finger-post decorated with a skull, and a witch's broomstick in the foreground. A work full of eye of newt and toe of frog, no doubt. He looked for *Right Royal Murder*, and took it down: a purple plush background, on which was placed the crown of England, stained with blood. An excellent cover, he thought, and a sure seller. Both Macpherson's and their star author had an eye for what would sell. He skimmed along the shelf for *Black Widow*. He missed it, and went back to read the thirty-odd titles methodically. There was none called *Black Widow*. He crossed over to an obscure corner of the room behind the door, where he had observed a serried mass of paperbacks and foreign editions. Here Sir Oliver had kept discreetly out of sight the more sensational editions of his works. Meredith went through them all, eventually having to get down on his hands and knees, there were so many. But there was no book called *Black Widow*.

Oliver Fairleigh seemed to have left his wife the copyright of a book that did not exist.

### CHAPTER IX

## FATHER AND SON

EMERGING FROM THE STUDY, with a feeling of having discovered something without having the slightest idea what, Inspector Meredith caught sight of the capable figure of Barbara Cozzens, purposefully cleaving a way from the servants' quarters to the stairs. The brief glimpse he had had of her when he had arrived had suggested to him that here was a woman with no nonsense about her – so much so, perhaps, as to be now and then an uncomfortable person to be with. She was dressed for the day after a death, in depressing dark brown skirt and severe-cut blouse. Her hair was pulled back into an exemplary bun, and her make-up was sparse and utterly unflamboyant. On the surface she looked like a shorthand-taking machine, and a totally conventional moral entity – but behind the glasses savage little glints of intelligence were to be detected.

'Oh, Miss Cozzens, I wondered if – '

'Of course, Inspector,' she said briskly, hardly even turning round; 'if you would like to come up to my office.'

The office, on the first floor, turned out to be a good-sized room – needed to be, in fact, because one wall was lined with filing cabinets, and there was an enormous old cupboard on the opposite side of the room, whose doors were hanging half open as if stuffed to the limits with manuscript, and aching to vomit some out. A quick glance from his darting eyes showed Meredith that this was indeed the case.

'I'm sorry to have to bother you, Miss Cozzens, when you must be very – '

'Oh, please don't bother with the preliminaries,

Inspector,' said Barbara Cozzens, gesturing him to the second chair and sitting down herself at the desk, as if he were all in a day's work. 'I haven't been Oliver Fairleigh's secretary all these years for nothing, you know. Slapdash he may have been, but inevitably one gained a few inklings of police procedure.'

'How many years, actually?'

'Six and a half. I've been responsible for his last seven novels and the eighth to come.'

'And lived here the whole time?'

'That's right. I have a very nice self-contained flat. I'm completely independent.'

Miss Cozzens seemed to insist on this. Was it to mark herself off from the domestic who 'lived in,' or to lay emphasis on the distance between herself and the family?

'I gather you were not at dinner last night?'

'No, indeed. It was a family affair – the birthday dinner always is. It was rather unusual for outsiders like the Woodstocks to be invited to it. As for myself, I have only dined with the family two or three times in the last few years. We saw more than enough of each other in the course of the day, more than enough. If I had been invited, I should not have gone.'

'Why?'

'I believe the birthday dinner was the day in the year when Sir Oliver felt that his position as paterfamilias gave him the right to be more than usually unbearable.'

Miss Cozzens's lips slapped together at this into a kind of smile. At Meredith's involuntary raising of the eyebrows, she seemed to sense disapproval, and went on: 'I'm being disloyal, do you think? But I think I'm safe in assuming that you will know a little about Sir Oliver's character and habits – either from the newspapers, or from local gossip. You will hear all about his relations with his family from somebody or other. As far as I'm concerned, the main thing is that you understand the situation at once, since it is obviously relevant to your enquiries.'

Frankness, then, was to be the order of the day. Meredith took the opportunity to ask her at once about the drinks cabinet.

'It was kept locked, at all times – both it and the one in the lounge. Because of Sir Mark, you know – a dipsomaniac, unfortunately.'

'But Sir Mark didn't live here.'

'No – but you could never tell when he might drop in. In search of alcohol, very often, when the pubs were closed. He was here last Sunday, for instance.'

'Was he now?' Meredith's Welsh intonation was suddenly very pronounced, and Barbara Cozzens had to get a grip on herself to stop herself from flinching.

'Yes, just in the afternoon. The Fairleighs had been out to lunch with the Woodstocks, whom you'll no doubt meet. Sir Oliver was rather pleased with himself when he came home, and he went to bed to have a rest – to contemplate his own superb destructiveness, I imagine. Mark saw his mother, and stayed around for a bit, but he heard that there was someone to dinner – Mr Simmington, from Sir Oliver's publishers – so he went away again at about half past six. I imagine he drove himself straight to a pub.'

'I see. But during his visit the drinks will have been locked away, I suppose?'

'Most definitely. They were *always* locked, and Sir Oliver kept the key. The only "strong drink" around was a bottle of sherry in the desk in the study: just now and then Sir Oliver treated himself to an extra glass – extra to Doctor Leighton's orders, that is. He imagined his wife noted the levels of the bottles, and kept this as a resource in emergencies. It was a polite fiction, in fact: both I and Lady Fairleigh knew about it.'

'You know that the decanter of lakka was poisoned?'

'From what I'd heard it sounded likely.' Miss Cozzens raised her eyebrows in a gesture of refined distaste. 'Really, a very melodramatic kind of murder. Quite like one of Sir Oliver's books!' And she shook her head in disapproval.

'Yes, indeed,' said Meredith meditatively: 'the toast,

the drinking, the collapse. Quite the stuff of detective stories. Was it any particular story you were thinking of?'

Miss Cozzens crinkled her brow – in thought, and perhaps in distaste. 'No, I don't think so. It's so difficult to remember: I do my best not to take much in while I take them down. But of course, when one has also to rough type them and then do the fair copy, one does inevitably get to know them. No, I don't think that any of the ones I've had to do with had any murder in them at all like that. In fact, Sir Oliver tended to avoid poison.'

'Why?'

'Dame Agatha used to do it so much better. In any case, it required too much research, and he was congenitally slothful. He preferred more direct, brutal methods.'

'I see. It's a pity. It did occur to me that someone – someone with a sense of humour – might have – '

'Used one of Sir Oliver's methods? Perfectly possible, of course. Though I have the gravest doubts whether any murderer using those books as a model would ever manage to kill anyone, let alone get away with it for any length of time.' Seeing Meredith smile appreciatively, Miss Cozzens preened herself on her sharp wit, and Meredith's quicksilver eyes saw her preening. In a second she was back to her business self. 'I'll go through all the novels at once, and see if there is anything reasonably close to what happened last night. After all, there are thirty or more, and I only know about ten or twelve at all well. What was the poison used?'

'Nicotine.'

'I see.' Miss Cozzens made a note of it. The murder, it seemed, had now been integrated into her office routine. 'I know his methods, so I should be able to skim through them quickly without actually having to read them.'

'Have you read one of his books called *Black Widow*?'

'*Black Widow*? There is no such novel.' Barbara Cozzens shook her head very definitely. 'I do all the financial side, you know – paperback rights, translations into foreign languages, all that kind of thing. So even if I haven't read them, I've got them all very clearly in my mind – how many times they've been reprinted, how much they've brought in, and so on. There is no book called *Black Widow*.'

'And yet it figures in his will.'

'Really? I don't understand?'

'He left *Foul Play At The Crossroads* to his son Terence – '

'Oh yes, a very profitable number, that.'

'*Right Royal Murder* to Bella – '

'The latest. That's going to be a goldmine – a real little goldmine.'

'And *Black Widow* to Lady Fairleigh-Stubbs.'

A flicker, Meredith could swear, went over Miss Cozzens's face, as if she was saying 'Then he must have left all the rest to Mark.' But it was immediately replaced by a furrowed brow, as she set her mind to the matter in hand. 'Well, he never used a pseudonym, so it can't be that. Wait – I know. It must be the one for publication after his death. No doubt that's it. He chose it for Lady Fairleigh because he knew it would bring in a nice little bit.'

'Do you mean the one he has just finished, or something?'

'Oh no, that's called *Murder Upstairs and Downstairs*. That was only finished last week, so it couldn't have figured in the will. No, this is one he held back. I believe he wrote it at some period when he was particularly productive – or facile, you might say. It was before my time, and I never heard what it was called. There were to be two of them – Sir Oliver's mind was very far from original – but he never got around to doing the second. People never think they're going to die, do they? And I'm sure Sir Oliver was convinced he could choose himself the time and manner of his going.'

'Where is the manuscript now?'

'At Macpherson's, I suppose. It's not here.' She waved her arms at the bulging, rickety cupboard. 'I have everything here, from first drafts to proof copies. He was always expecting some American library to offer for them, and none ever did. It may look chaotic, but I know perfectly well everything that's there.' She thought for a moment. 'Of course, it's just possible it's in the study.'

'Wouldn't you know about it?'

'Not necessarily. This room is mine – my office. The study was Sir Oliver's. I was called in there, to be recording angel when inspiration struck, usually between eleven and one in the morning.' Her lips again slapped together in a brief, sharp smile. 'But we kept to our own areas: I found out very early that this was the only way to keep the peace. And in fact it would have been more than my life was worth to poke around in the study.'

'Well, I'll look around and make enquiries. No doubt it's a blind alley, but it seemed an oddity worth looking into. It will be interesting in any case to talk to his publishers.'

'Mr Simmington is very intelligent. Knew how to handle Sir Oliver. It's an art one had to develop over the years.'

Inspector Meredith had risen. From the window he saw the eldest son of the victim wandering down from the terrace into the gardens of the house that was now his. 'I've no doubt it was an art,' he said. 'And Sir Mark, I gather, didn't have it.'

'No, indeed. If anything he deliberately provoked him.'

'One last question,' said Meredith, turning quickly round again to Miss Cozzens and surprising a look of reluctant admiration of Mark's attitude on her face. 'Can you tell me who had the best chance of getting at the drinks cupboard in the study?'

Miss Cozzens thought: 'Surtees, of course. He was sometimes given the key. Otherwise, I suppose you'd have had to steal the key while Sir Oliver was asleep. Which wouldn't be easy, because he locked his door.' She looked with Meredith down to the gardens below. 'I'll tell you one thing. The person least likely to have been able to get hold of it was Sir Mark.'

Meredith gazed with her at the lonely strolling figure. 'That's the conclusion I've come to,' he said regretfully.

The day was warm rather than hot, and the shadows were already beginning to lengthen when Meredith slipped out of a side door and went in the direction he had seen Mark take. The grounds of Wycherley Court were extensive, and undoubtedly gentlemanly. They had never, it seemed, been allowed to go to waste. Meredith (who had been born in the county and whose Welsh accent was an inheritance from his parents, cherished zealously out of some obscure feelings of tribal loyalty) remembered when the estate had been sold by the Hattersleys – local squires from time fairly immemorial, who had been early in the emigration of their class to enjoy the benefits of birching and low taxation on the Isle of Man. That was about '50-'51, he guessed, and even then the property as a whole was in fairly good shape. Much care had gone into the grounds since then, and much love. Meredith noted a gardener leaning on a spade with an unmistakable air of waiting for knocking-off time. The love, he presumed, had come from Lady Fairleigh.

He found Mark in a little clearing on the far corner of the estate, almost surrounded by elms, which were casting long accusatory fingers of shadow towards the house. He was sitting on a seat, deep in thought, but not too deep to hear Meredith's approach.

'I am sorry, Inspector,' he said, getting up eagerly. 'I do apologize. I should have realized you would want to see me. I'd no intention of making you come to search me out.'

His manner, like his words, was apologetic, but it was oddly confident too. His apology was the apology of a man who was quite consciously in charge. Suddenly his air was that of the public-school prefect, grown up. Meredith shot one of his quick glances at the face: good-looking, rather full about the lips, the eye rather dulled. It was an oddly unformed face for a man in his mid-twenties: it was a face from which one might have expected almost anything.

'We can talk here as well as anywhere,' said Meredith, perching bird-like on the long park bench, and looking at Mark with his guileless, confidential smile. 'Until my lab boys start getting reports through I can't do much more than go around feeling my way. They're the ones who do all the work these days.'

'But still, you do know it was murder?'

'We know he was poisoned. Nicotine poison. In the decanter.'

'Poor Mother,' said Mark simply. He sat for a few moments, apparently genuinely upset. He took out a packet of cigarettes, put one in his mouth and lit it. Suddenly Meredith realized that his hand was shaking. 'Nicotine,' he said, with an obvious effort to be cool. 'I don't know anything about poisons. Is that a common one?'

'To murder someone with? Not very. But it's easy enough to obtain if you know the way.'

'Poor Mother,' said Mark again, his voice more normal. 'All those years putting up with Father, and they end like this.' He paused, and then said: 'The press is going to be absolutely foul.'

There was a note of strong feeling in his voice which intrigued Meredith, so he said: 'You have had experience of the press?'

'Some,' said Mark. His voice was very quiet. He seemed to be surveying the experiences of his last years as if they were someone else's. 'Father attracted reporters like flies to a honey jar. I was the little blob of honey on the plate that got a few stray flies. You can imagine the sort of thing they said about me: first it was "fast living," "devil-may-care," then it was "ne'er-do-well," then it was – well, you can imagine. I was never interesting enough for more than a line or two here and there, but still – yes, I've had more than enough of reporters.'

'The police are supposed to work in with the press these days,' said Meredith. 'And real little blabber-mouths some of us have become, too. But I find, personally, that the best policy is usually to say nothing at all.'

'I was not always in a condition to say nothing at all,' said Mark. His hand, though resting on the arm of the seat, was not quite still. Meredith felt that they were getting on to difficult territory, and tiptoed cautiously on.

'It was lucky for you, at any rate, that you were drunk last night,' he said. Mark looked at him, a direct, troubled look.

'Yes, wasn't it?' he said. 'It's odd to think of myself there – present in the body, absent in the mind. I've been like that often enough before, but nothing quite like that has happened while I've been out.'

'Why do you think your brother and your sister took you across to the study?'

'Considerate of them, wasn't it?' Mark's answer came quickly and bitterly. Then he paused and thought for a little. 'That's for you to decide. I suppose they'd say they wanted me to be in on the carefree jollity of a birthday dinner at Wycherley Court.'

'And you would say?'

There was a long silence now. 'Perhaps they would be quite pleased to have me there, for the finger of scorn to be pointed at,' said Mark at last.

'There is another, even less pleasant possibility,' said Meredith.

'Of course there is,' said Mark loudly, apparently genuinely agitated. 'But they are my brother and sister. You don't expect me calmly to chew over with you the possibility of their being – what's the word? – parricides, do you, nicely weighing the pros and cons? It's for you to find out.'

'Of course I don't expect you to do that,' said Meredith, very charming. 'But I have to consider the possibilities, and I've no doubt you will do the same. They (or one of them) may have wanted you there because they hoped you would come round. They may have been banking on the fact that you would be with the rest when the presents were opened, so that we could imagine you, while the rest of the party's attention was diverted, slipping the poison into the decanter. It must be obvious that in any other circumstances you would be prime suspect, in view of your performance at the Prince Albert in Hadley last weekend.'

'Ah, you know about that?'

'I suspect everyone in the area knows about it. I shall make some enquiries about when the gossip started in Wycherley, and when people in the house got to know, but I think you can assume that everyone at the birthday party had heard of it.'

'Odd, that – I don't remember much about it myself. Well, if that was Terence or Bella's little plan, it rather misfired, didn't it?'

'Yes, if it was, it did,' said Meredith non-committally. Then he turned directly to Mark and asked: 'How long have you been drinking so heavily, sir?'

'Oh years – years and years. When I was seventeen or eighteen I used to go on occasional benders. From about twenty onwards I've needed it. I need it at this moment.'

'But you're not taking it?'

'No.' There was a brief silence. 'I feel I need my wits about me. You're implying I could have been intended as – what's the word? – a fall guy. I had the same idea, in the back of my mind. In any case, I don't know what's going on, and I need all the cool thinking I can manage to find out.' Suddenly his brow unfurrowed. 'And you know, coming into all this makes a difference.' He waved his hand around the estates stretching like a *Country Life* illustration towards the house, mellow and golden in the distance.

'In what way, sir?'

'In every way. It means I own something. It means I have a stable base, and a way of life mapped out. It means responsibilities, decisions, something solid to do. I don't know whether Father realized it, but it does make a difference.' He paused again, as if the interview with Meredith was part of a heavy session of self-communion which had gone on before he came, and would go on after he left. 'If you want to put it crudely, you could say it makes all the difference that he is dead.'

'You drank because he was alive?'

'Oh yes, that's certainly true. Because I knew that by drinking I would be disappointing him, ruining his plans for me, embarrassing him – in so far as that was possible. I've always been conscious of him, in the background: he's been with me every minute of the day, ever since I can remember.'

The brooding look in the eyes – troubled, turbulent – was that of a man not naturally introspective, trying to come to terms with his own situation.

'You drank because he hated you?' hazarded Meredith, optimistically putting the verb in the past tense. Mark turned, and his expression had changed, lightened, become almost one of wonder.

'Do you know, Inspector, I don't believe he did.'

CHAPTER X

## MASTER AND MAN

AT MEREDITH's look of surprise, Mark waved his hand deprecatingly: 'Of course, that sounded a bit silly, in view of everything that's gone on between us. And I don't even mean we had a love-hate relationship, either. It's practically impossible to explain what I *do* mean to someone who didn't know Father personally.'

'I'm getting a picture,' said Meredith.

'Yes, but is it the right one – or rather, is the emphasis right? There was the monster that the newspapers made of him, or rather that he made of himself for the newspapers' benefit. Everyone around here can tell you a story based on this monster, and quite a few of them will actually be true. But the important thing is that he was *performing* this role – and enjoying the performance, of course. And this was always true, whatever he did, whatever mood he was in. Last night he'd promised Bella to be good for the birthday dinner, and through the haze I can remember what he was like when I arrived, and when we were having drinks before dinner: he wasn't *being nice*, he was *performing* being nice – a galumphing, hearty *performance*. He was being the stage squire in a William Douglas Home play. And the point about Father was that he loved roles, all sorts of roles. And if you presented him with a possible one, he grabbed it with both hands, and hammed it up to the skies.'

Mark, as if surprised at his own eloquence and insight, suddenly came to a halt, and looked anxiously at Meredith to see if he had understood. Meredith digested the notion slowly. He was wondering whether the picture was a true one, and wondering too what had given this rather ordinary boy such an acute perception.

'So you mean,' he said, 'that you, by being – what shall we say? – unsatisfactory, presented him with a role?'

'Exactly.' Mark flung himself back in his seat, and made odd sketching motions with his hands in the air that seemed to be an outline of Oliver Fairleigh's bull-frog body. 'A plum role, handed him on a plate: heavy father; outraged Victorian parent; disappointed head of a noble family. Not just a lovely part, but tailor-made for him. And he played it up to the hilt, enjoying every minute.'

'But you think he didn't actually feel anything, any hatred or outrage?'

'That's what I've come to think.' Mark crossed his legs, and turned towards Meredith, like a salesman trying to put over a product. 'I don't think Father *felt* very much at all. He was fond of Bella, in his way. Perhaps of Mother too, though he would never have moved a muscle of his body out of consideration for *her* feelings. Beyond that, there was only himself, his comfort and convenience, fending off the boredom of life, creating fuss and kerfuffle, getting into the news, bullying and embarrassing people to *prove* himself in some way or other. But about me, I don't think he felt anything, one way or another – nothing you could analyse and say, "This is sincere." '

'You've obviously thought about it a lot.'

'I have. And I'm not sure I quite saw it like this yesterday, even. But that's how I think it was.'

'And where does this leave you, sir?'

'In what way?'

'Did *you* hate *him*?'

'Yes, oh yes.' There was no sign of reserve or hesitation as Mark stretched back in the seat and admitted this. 'I hated his selfishness, his cruelty, his ludicrous snobbery, his publicity-seeking – I hated everything about him. But in the end it may all come back to egotism on my part: I hated him because I sensed he felt nothing about me as a person. Nothing at all. Wasn't conscious of me, and couldn't care less. He made me cringe with loathing.'

The two men sat silent for a moment. Into the silence came an odd sound, like an asthmatic barrel-organ tuning up. Across the clearing, waddling, came Cuff, snuffling along with his nose obsessively to the ground, his dim eyes winking with effort. At length he arrived at the seat, smelt in a leisurely, scientific manner up Mark's trouser leg, then with a great grunt of achievement flopped his ungainly body down at his feet and went to sleep.

'The first defector to the new master,' said Mark. He did not sound displeased.

'How have you lived, since you left school?' asked Meredith, unwilling to let the subject of Mark's misspent years drop.

'I went up to Oxford when I was nineteen. Father said it had to be Balliol or Christ Church, and I just scraped into Christ Church – mainly due to Dad's giving them a collection of early eighteenth-century pamphlets for the library a year or so before I tried my luck. He liked doing deals on that sort of level: he used to say it was impossible to underestimate the power of self-interest.'

'But you didn't take your degree?'

'Good Lord, no. I didn't last more than a term and a half. I was sent down for idleness and drunkenness.' He threw a wry smile in Meredith's direction: 'You had to be *very* idle, and *very* drunken to be sent down from The House.'

'And after that?'

'Well, as I realize now, Oxford was just a period of trying my wings away from the parental shadow. After that I went on and on and down and down. The City – out. Agricultural College – out. Australia – I flew back after two and a half weeks, paying my fare with a cheque that bounced. Since then – well, whatever I felt would humiliate him most. Door-to-door salesman in ladies' underwear; chucker-out at a Soho club – only the people I had to chuck out were tougher than I was, and not so drunk. Let's see, what else? Oh, I worked behind the counter on the ground floor in Fortnum's – Dad came in and saw me, and had to be carried in to the manager's office. Then odds and sods here and there: salesman, rep, commission agent – you know the kind of thing. In fact, you name it, I've done it.'

'Was it all done as a sort of revenge against your father?'

'I think so. I've tried to pull myself together and make a go of something now and again, but the thought of his condescension or his sneers always sent me off again. If I ever make a go of anything in the future, it will be because he isn't around to coin witticisms and throw them in my direction when there are plenty of people around to hear.'

'Ever been in trouble with the police?' asked Meredith, knowing very well he had.

'Drunken driving, bad debts, disorderly behaviour,' said Mark promptly. 'As I'm sure you know only too well, Inspector.' Meredith decided it would be as well not to underestimate Mark. He was, at any rate, too intelligent to be played with. But a flicker had crossed his eyes as he recited his offences. Had there, conceivably, been something else?

'Your father had to pay the debts, I suppose?' he said.

'Frequently. Less so of late. People have been getting wise – and he put a notice in *The Times* disclaiming responsibility. So credit has been tough for the last year or so.'

'And your mother has helped you too?'

'Oh, Mother is a brick. But she's no fool, either. She's always been good for a small touch, but after the first couple of times she drew a firm line, and stuck to it. Anyway, I always thought it was more fun to get it out of Father.'

'Knowing it would come to you in the end anyway?'

Mark paused before he replied, as if it might be a trap. 'Suspecting that it would.'

'Because he would want the money and estate to go together with the title?'

'Yes, that's what I guessed. Which is pretty funny when you think of the title.' When Meredith raised his crescent eyebrows, Mark just said: 'Ask Mum about it. She's very good on the subject when Dad isn't around to hear her.' He stopped, and smiled, very naturally. 'As, of course, he isn't.'

'Well, well,' said Meredith, stretching his legs, 'I must be getting back to see what has come up. One last question: did you have a duplicate key to the drinks cabinet in the study?'

'Of course I didn't, Inspector. You'd have been questioning me in a very different tone of voice if you thought that possible.' Mark smiled confidently, got up, and the two strolled towards the house – Cuff scrambling to his feet and following cumbrously behind them, sighing noisily at the restlessness of humankind. 'As you know,' Mark went on, 'the locks were to keep me out. Though as time went on they also became a sort of symbol that Dad was to cut down himself. But if I had got hold of a duplicate – and I did sound Surtees out, believe me – the locks would have been changed. The amount I drink would have been noted, and Dad certainly wasn't the sort you could fool by watering down.'

'You weren't offered a drink last Sunday?'

'Last Sunday? Was I here then?' He puzzled a little. 'Yes, I think I remember. I dropped in while the pubs were shut, since I was in the area. Sunday's a horrible day for a man with a thirst. But Dad was asleep, and Mum couldn't have given me anything even if she'd wanted to. I stayed around for a bit, but I'd had pretty much, and I get gloomy, and it wasn't much fun for Mum. I might have stopped for dinner, but someone was coming, and I knew Dad would perform for the visitors – aim a few hob-nailed witticisms at me, and so on. So I sloped off.'

'When?'

'About six, I should think. Ask Mum.' Mark turned and looked straight at him. 'Anyway, Father hadn't come down by then. None of the drinks cabinets had been opened. And I didn't come back. Is that quite clear?'

'Do you remember where you were that evening?'

'No, I don't, frankly. But it must have been the Thistle here in Wycherley, or the Horse and Groom at Oakden. I know I didn't drive far, and those are my two usual haunts. If you check there someone should remember. I usually make myself conspicuous.'

As they approached the house (Cuff's breathing becoming ever more stentorian, a heavy performance in the Oliver Fairleigh manner, probably to indicate that he preferred a master with more sedentary habits) there emerged from the conservatory at the corner of the house the figure of Surtees. He had obviously observed their approach. There was something about the set of his shoulders, about the way he carried himself, that marked an indefinable shift from the Surtees Meredith had talked to earlier in the afternoon. There was a loss of swagger, of bounce.

'Excuse me, Sir Mark,' he said softly as he came up –

whether the softness was of insinuation, or a gesture of respect to a house in mourning was not obvious – 'I wondered if you would like anything special tonight in the way of wine.'

It was the sort of moment, historically sweet, when the scapegrace Prince of Wales stands to receive the crooked knees and courtly kisses of the mourners round a royal death-bed, when he sees the favourites and flunkies who have carried stories of his excesses to the parental ear suddenly acknowledge a shift in power. Instead of the sceptre and the great seal, Mark had been granted the keys to the wine-cellar and the drinks cupboard. He would have been less than human if he had not relished the situation, though only the briefest of smiles crossed his lips.

'It's hardly a day for celebration,' he said coolly. 'We can have the Médoc.'

'Of course, Sir Mark. And would you like your clothes laid out for dinner?'

'My clothes are not the sort that are laid out,' said Mark. 'No, thank you.'

Surtees turned and went back towards the conservatory, the set of his shoulders once more eloquent: he was not altogether satisfied. Mark, having watched him, resumed his walk along the path round to the front of the house, his full mouth once more indulging in a tiny smile.

'Surtees has heard about the will,' he said to Meredith. 'I wonder how.'

'These things get around,' said Meredith. 'I'm afraid I may have said something to Miss Cozzens that could have given her a clue.'

'Miss Cozzens?' said Mark. 'How odd. I wouldn't have thought she was the type who would let herself gossip with the servants. I'm not well up with the various leagues and alliances in this house.' He paused, put his hands on his hips, and surveyed the manor house, glowing in the late sun. 'Not that I will need to be. The regular staff will have to be cut more or less to nothing, and we'll rely on getting help from the village.'

'I'm surprised Surtees bothers to ingratiate himself,' said Meredith. 'It's not as though he's likely to find himself at the Labour Exchange. People in his line can practically name their price today. It seems he wants to stay on.'

'I wondered at that myself,' said Mark. 'I expect it's Bella. It usually is Bella, you know. And probably it's Bella who has told him about the will. But in any case, he's batting on a very poor wicket. Whatever happens, Surtees is going to go. I'm looking forward to giving him his notice personally.'

The two men walked up the front steps. Today Mark did not stumble on the last one. The smile was still on his face as he contemplated getting rid of Surtees. Before going in he turned and looked down the drive, curving towards the main gate. It was closed, and on either side of it stood a massive police constable. Outside, on the little country road were several cars and little knots of reporters with cameras. Most of them were in the act of photographing the new master of Wycherley Court, at the entrance to his stately home.

'The vultures are gathering,' said Mark, the smile disappearing from his face. 'I suppose it will be up to you to provide them with carrion, Inspector.'

He turned, and went quickly into the house.

Dinner was hardly a more comfortable meal than lunch, and the presence of Bella did nothing to improve matters. The passion of the morning was – to all appearances – over and had been replaced by a new ice age. Her dress, without being flashy, nevertheless made none of the usual concessions to the custom of mourning. But once more she had made herself into a beautiful object, untouchable. For much of the meal she sat in total silence.

Otherwise the pattern of lunch repeated itself. Mark drank a glass of wine. Terence drank decidedly more. His long fair hair was beginning to look heavy and lank; his face was shiny, sweaty, as if he had forgotten to wash. The conversation was carried on, when at all, by Mark and his mother. He had talked to her before dinner, telling her of Meredith's confirmation that there had been poison in the decanter. Once the suspicion that she had been fighting against was confirmed, Lady Fairleigh seemed to give a great sigh and accept the matter, though there was a sad lethargy about her, as if she could now only expect worse and worse to come. But the presence of the other children at dinner made her make some efforts to pretend normality.

'The Woodstocks rang earlier,' she said, addressing her remarks to Bella. 'They were very kind, of course. They offered us any help we might need.'

'Really?' said Bella. 'It's difficult to think what help either of those two could give.' She returned to her food, seeming hungry.

When Surtees came round with the sweet, Mark had the impression that he was trying to catch Bella's eye. If he was, he failed. Bella remained in her envelope of ice, staring contemptuously ahead of her.

'I'll put the coffee in the lounge, sir, is that all right?' said Surtees, bending by Mark's ear. Mark nodded.

'Enjoying these little marks of respect, Mark?' asked Terence in a thick, unpleasant voice.

'I am, rather,' returned Mark levelly. 'I shall have to while they last, because it won't be long. Naturally we shall be cutting down on staff here.'

'Why?' said Bella sharply. Then, as if she had revealed something, she cut her voice down to its usual drawl and said contemptuously: 'There's no reason to, is there? The royalties will be coming in as usual.'

'Except of course,' said Mark, 'that I shan't be writing a book a year to keep the flow going.' The thought didn't seem to have occurred to Bella, and he elaborated: 'One profession I do not think of entering is the mystery-writing trade.'

'I hope things won't be too hard for you,' said Bella, the

cut of the voice making up for the heaviness of the irony. 'I wouldn't want you to miss the royalties from my little legacy.'

'What an appropriate word, royalties,' murmured her mother, whom family disagreements tended to send into fatuities. 'In view of the subject-matter,' she added feebly.

'I think you should be very happy with *Right Royal Murder*,' said Mark, unruffled. 'The Jubilee will soon be over, but probably every royal wedding and birth will lead to a reprint. And heaven knows, there are likely to be plenty of them.'

'Thanks,' said Bella.

'Shall we have coffee?' said Mark, rising. By now his face was a little flushed from the effort of not drinking and maintaining conversation. Not being able to think of any way of asserting themselves, Terence and Bella trailed along to the sitting-room.

Coffee was set on a side-table, and the drinks cabinet stood open. The liqueurs from the study had of course been commanded by the police, but replacements had been brought up, and several bottles of spirits had also been set out by Surtees in a tempting array. Is it a bribe, thought Mark, or an invitation?

'Will you pour, Mother?' he said.

'I'll have a whisky,' said Terence.

'Terence!' said his mother.

'Of course, Terence,' said Mark, going over and taking up the bottle in his hand. 'Anything with it?'

'Neat,' said Terence.

'Mark, please don't give it to him!'

'Terence has had a bad day, Mother,' said Mark quietly. 'I'm sure it will do him good.' He poured into the glass a good stiff measure. 'Anyway there are far worse things than whisky, aren't there, Terence?' He straightened himself, the bottle still in his hands, and looked straight at his brother. 'Drugs, for instance.'

Mark still stood, his hands automatically screwing on the cap, looking at his brother and sister. Terence's face, already fiery, seemed to grow purple and crumple. Bella's eyes opened wide, and she seemed about to say something to her younger brother. Lady Fairleigh, arrested in the act of pouring, looked from one to the other, her eyes clouded with bewilderment.

'There you are, Terence,' said Mark, going over. 'Oh dear, Mother, is that my coffee? I think you'd better pour me another, if you don't mind.'

Lady Fairleigh looked down, and found a dark pool of coffee covering the whole tray.

CHAPTER XI

BARABBAS

FROM *The Times*, obituary page. Monday 19 June 1977.

## OLIVER FAIRLEIGH

The death was announced early yesterday morning of Sir Oliver Fairleigh-Stubbs, Bart, MBE, better known as Oliver Fairleigh, the mystery writer.

Oliver Fairleigh-Stubbs was born on 17 June, 1912, the only son of Frederick Fairleigh-Stubbs of Birmingham, a manufacturer of kitchenware. He was brought up in the richly independent atmosphere of a provincial industrial city, and the prosperity of the family firm was greatly augmented when it shifted to war production during the years 1914-1918. However, although his father received a baronetcy in the new year's honours list for 1922, the Fairleigh-Stubbs works did not easily weather the transition to peace-time production, and went bankrupt in 1925. It was no doubt due to the economic difficulties of the family that Oliver Fairleigh did not go to university, a loss which he never regretted.

The first years of his working life (1932-1940) were spent in journalism, initially with the *Birmingham Post*, later on Fleet Street with the *Daily Clarion*. His politics at this time were the conventional blend of idealism and socialism, and his witty and trenchant reviews in the *Clarion* won him entry into the circle surrounding Auden and Isherwood. The war, however, led to a change of direction both in his career and in his politics. He served in North Africa and Italy, proving an effective if idiosyncratic soldier. In his spare time he wrote his first detective novel, *Murder by Debrett*, and the publication of this in November 1945 marked the beginning of a series of highly entertaining stories, distinctive for their narrative pace and their mild and harmless snob appeal.

His politics, in contrast to those of many of his fellow soldiers, had moved sharply to the right. In 1947 he stood as Conservative candidate at a by-election in the Milton Grove constituency of Sheffield, but his personality proved ill-adapted to the democratic give-and-take of the hustings. In later years his pronouncements on political and social matters grew more and more extreme (a much quoted article for the *People* on the cult of the Angry Young Man was a case in point), but these were part of the elaborate public persona which Oliver Fairleigh (with the delighted co-operation of Fleet Street) built up over the years. By a series of *obiter dicta* and escapades he impressed himself on the public as a formidable upholder of Victorian attitudes, a country gentleman of the old school who had appointed himself the scourge of modernity in all its forms. The publicity he gained did no harm to the sales of the stream of works which poured from his pen, and at his death he was unquestionably the most popular writer of this kind of fiction in the English-speaking world.

Lacking the literary pretensions of a Sayers, or the ingenuity of a Christie, his stories are notable for their erratic high-spirits and unfailing readability. Among the most accomplished, perhaps, are *Murder By Degrees*, with its unkind if entertaining picture of a Cambridge College, *Skirting Death*, the first of the Mrs Merrydale books, and *Foul Play At The Crossroads*, in which to the conventional formula is added a spice of *grand guignol*.

In 1949 Sir Oliver Fairleigh-Stubbs (as he had by then become, on the death of his father in 1946) married Eleanor, daughter of the Hon. Philip Erskine Howard. There were two sons and one daughter of the marriage, of which the elder son, Mark, succeeds to the baronetcy.

The obituary of Oliver Fairleigh, spread over two columns extended nearly down to the middle of the page. Underneath (testifying to the change of values that had come over Printing House Square in the later years of Oliver Fairleigh's life) were short obituaries of a Scottish Bishop and a cabinet minister in the second Attlee government. In the centre of the obituary was a photograph of Oliver Fairleigh. He stared out on the public at large, outraged, apoplectic, incredulous. Public folly, it seemed, had driven him to the verge of insanity. He looked like a Crimean War general whose men had deserted en masse, leaving him to face alone a regiment of galloping Cossacks. Not for the first time in his career, Meredith, sitting on the early morning train from Hadley to London, felt glad that the murder victim was indeed the victim, not one of the living suspects.

Turning to page two, he found a brief and neutrally worded announcement that the police were investigating the circumstances in which the novelist Oliver Fairleigh had died.

The offices of Macpherson's the publishers were in the West End of London – an area of parks and clubs, of royal palaces and exclusive hotels, of idiosyncratic shops which remained in existence against the logic and economics of the nineteen-seventies. They were, in fact, in Oliver Fairleigh country.

The building was Queen Anne, and in spite of all the efforts of a modern construction company to halt the sinkings and slidings that Time afflicts such buildings with, it was dark, irregular and undeniably quaint. It had all the air of an old family firm, and was therefore much approved by Oliver Fairleigh; but in fact its origins (like his) were late nineteenth-century and were based on the business acumen of its Scottish founder (a small printer of great thrift, industry and intransigence). The firm had published a series of volumes of popular education which just matched the needs of the post-1870 generation of board-school products. Now they were a firm of great respectability and even greater prosperity. People in the trade laughed at their love of a best-seller – and silently ground their teeth at their skill in finding them.

Inspector Meredith arrived there by appointment at nine-thirty, and stood in the high room with the sagging ceiling which was its main office. Here a decorative young lady played with a typewriter and met the general public, while a fearsome old dragon, face to the wall, did all the real work. Meredith sent his name up to Mr Gerald Simmington, but when footsteps clattered down the sounding wooden stairway there were four feet to be distinguished. He realized as soon as the first man came into the room that he was being given the red carpet treatment. This could only be Sir Edwin Macpherson.

Sir Edwin was very large: not a fat, forceful man like Oliver Fairleigh, but a stupendously gross, flabby, hearty man, whose trousers were a great pin-striped chalice for holding paunch and buttocks in. It was miraculous how two little legs could hold up so much body. He was a man of multiple chins and bags under his eyes like chandeliers, a man of cigars and port-wine laugh, very jolly, hail-fellow, with a clear eye for the main chance and a quick profit. Gerald Simmington was a sandy-haired young man in his early thirties who kept, and seemed to belong, in the background.

Sir Edwin's demeanour on this occasion was an attempt

at gravity – gravity mingled with discretion. The observer
got the idea, though, that given the tiniest of openings,
cheerfulness would break through.

'Sad business, Inspector, terribly sad business,' he said
as he sighted the raincoated figure in the corner of the
office and advanced with outstretched hand. 'A great
character, you know, a wonderfully vivid personality. A
national figure, you might say. One of the old school, of
course – nobody like him these days. We shall feel his loss
here, you know – feel it deeply.' At these words Meredith
noted the typing dragon in the corner half-turn from
contemplating the wall and eye disapprovingly the enormous back of her employer: her expression suggested she
was calling down on him the wrath of God for his menda-
city. 'Anyway, thought I should come down and see you
myself, before you talk to Gerald here. Assure you we want
to do everything we can to help. Just ask, and the whole
staff's at your beck and call. Appalling way for a man like
him to go – monstrous, almost like a bad joke. He was our
most popular author you know, by a long chalk. So if we
can help you, we'll pull out all the stops, eh Gerald?'

'Was Sir Oliver liked here?' asked Meredith conversationally (for it seemed that Sir Edwin's purpose in
coming down was conversation, rather than making
himself available for questions).

'Liked?' boomed the great voice, as if the question was
so absurd as to release him from the need for gravity.
'Liked? Good heavens no. He didn't want to be liked,
Oliver Fairleigh. He wanted to be feared.' The great laugh
rang out, echoing against the sagging ceiling. 'And we
were all scared stiff of him. I too! I most of all!' The laugh
boomed out again, then stopped suddenly as Sir Edwin
seemed to recollect the situation.

'He was in here last week, wasn't he?' asked Meredith.

'Yes. When was it, now?' A murmured prompt came
from Simmington behind the bulwark of back. 'That's
right, Tuesday. We had lunch at the Savoy. Had to go
along myself this time, because I'd skipped his last few

visits here. Try and avoid them if I can – too embarrassing for a quiet chap like me. Still, he was in a frightfully good mood for him, wasn't he Gerald? Didn't shout at the waiter till coffee came.'

'Do you know why he was in a good mood?'

'He'd been at the BBC during the morning, and thoroughly enjoyed himself.' Sir Edwin chuckled fruitily. 'Been a naughty boy, as usual. That was always the way with old Oliver: if you could get him just after he'd done something outrageous, he could be as nice as pie.'

'I think I heard something about this BBC episode,' said Meredith. 'There was a piece in one of the papers last week – in the gossip columns. Wasn't he insulting about other crime writers?'

'Something of the sort, I believe. Didn't specify, though: just mentioned senile hacks and so on. We've had trouble over that, I can assure you.' The great laugh rang out again. 'You know our Golden Dagger series? Well half the people who write for that seem to have heard about it and assumed it was an insult to them personally. Rum lot, writers. Told Gerald to tell them if they were senile or were hacks, we wouldn't be publishing them. Hope they believed it. Everyone loves flattery, and when it comes to writers, you should lay it on with a trowel!'

'It's an interesting line of enquiry,' said Meredith, trying to respond in kind to Sir Edwin's merriment. 'Perhaps one of them did it, out of revenge. Or perhaps there was a whole conspiracy of crime writers.'

This set Sir Edwin off. 'A conspiracy of crime writers! You've quite a turn of phrase, Inspector! I can just imagine them all getting together to plan it! Sounds like a bad Hollywood film, eh?' He sobered down suddenly. 'Mustn't joke. They're our authors. So was poor old Oliver, with all his faults. We'll miss his books once a year. We've lots better, but none as popular, eh Gerald?' And he wagged a few chins in the direction of his shadow, and mentally contemplated his future sales figures.

'Well, I mustn't keep you,' he said finally, giving the

impression he meant 'you mustn't keep me.' 'Gerald will take care of you. Come to us. Any hour of the day or night. Dreadful business, dreadful business.' At the door he paused, thoughtfully. 'Publicity isn't doing us any harm, though,' he said, and marched away up the sounding stairs.

'Perhaps you'd like to come to my office,' murmured Gerald Simmington, sounding like a harp solo after a Sousa march. He led the way along a labyrinth of narrow corridors, strategically interspersed with steps to trip or tumble. Finally they arrived at a little room, neatly stacked with books and files, with a dirty window over-looking the arid well that was the area, and a desk of exemplary tidiness.

'I find if I don't keep it in apple-pie order I'm over-whelmed with paper in a matter of hours,' said Gerald Simmington, as if some explanation were demanded. He gestured Meredith to a chair, and sat down himself. His elbows, apart, rested on the desk, but his long fingers came delicately together under his chin, as if he were trying to make himself into a neat geometrical pattern. 'As you know,' he said in his courteous, neutral voice, 'we've published all the Oliver Fairleigh books here, so over the years we've certainly got to know his – little ways, shall we say? I'm not sure how else we can help you, but perhaps you'd better tell me that.'

He blinked rather formally behind his heavy spectacles. A born second-in-command, thought Meredith.

'I wanted to ask you,' he said, 'about your dinner with Sir Oliver the Sunday before last.'

'Oh yes. It was my first real visit there, you know. He knew I was in the area, and asked me to dinner. I was apprehensive, of course, but it went off very nicely. I gather he'd been out to lunch and made everybody grovel, and – as Sir Edwin suggested a moment ago – that did tend to put him in a good humour for the rest of the day. We discussed the new book, *Murder Upstairs and Downstairs*. He was very late with it, but we here had decided to hurry it through and get it out by early October.'

'What I was really interested in,' said Meredith, 'was the drinks: did you have liqueurs with coffee after dinner?'

'Yes, we did. Just Sir Oliver and I – Lady Fairleigh said she was tired. We went into the study.'

'Did Sir Oliver drink lakka?'

'Yes, he did. Was it – ?'

'Yes, it was.'

Mr Simmington's colourless face lost some of its minor-civil-servant's anonymity, and seemed to evince a spark of interest. 'Well, well,' he said, leaning back in his chair. 'I've been editing the Golden Dagger series for four years, and this is the first time I've encountered a real murder.' It didn't seem to upset him.

'When you went into the study, was the cabinet with the liqueurs in already unlocked?'

'No, Sir Oliver unlocked it himself.'

'And afterwards?'

'He locked it himself as I got up to leave. He was very particular about it, and I noticed it specially.'

'Why did you notice it?'

'Well, to tell you the truth, I'd heard rumours about his son, and I wondered whether that was the reason.'

'I see,' said Meredith. He grinned. 'You make it very difficult.'

'I'm sorry? Why is that?'

'I'm trying to establish *when* the decanter could have been tampered with. It could have been done immediately before Sir Oliver drank, in which case my list of suspects is everybody who was in the room, except one.'

'One?'

'Mark, the elder son, was too drunk. Out like a light as far as I can see, and nobody even hints he could have got up and sneaked over. On the other hand, to do it then would be extremely risky: it would need nerves of iron. The alternative is, it could have been done before –

which would significantly widen our list of suspects. The problem is how anyone could have got hold of the keys.'

'You mean Sir Oliver kept them with him the whole time?'

'That seems to be the general testimony. That would make it very difficult, almost impossible, except that he sometimes gave them to Surtees, his man, which opens up certain possibilities. What I'm wondering about at the moment is whether Sir Oliver was really as careful as people make out, and I was hoping that, for example, he might have left the cabinet open while he saw you out.'

Mr Simmington blinked again, and remained sunk in anaemic thought for a few seconds. 'I'm sorry, Inspector, but it was as I said. He definitely locked up before we left the study. But of course, he drank a lot – as a general rule, I mean. Very likely some other time during the week he could have forgotten to lock it.'

Meredith shook his head. 'There again, that seems ruled out. Apparently he only drank liqueurs at weekends. Some sort of compromise with doctor's orders, I believe.'

Mr Simmington shook his sandy head dubiously. 'Well, I'm surprised to hear it. I wouldn't have thought Oliver Fairleigh had so much self-discipline. I must say he always struck me as a man who would do exactly what he wanted to do – and damn the consequences.'

'Yes,' agreed Meredith, 'that's the impression the various accounts of him have made on me. But still, people seem to agree that by and large he stuck to his regime. How many glasses of lakka did he have?'

'Just the one, I think.'

'And you didn't leave the study at any time?'

'No, we neither of us left it. I wasn't there for any length of time because frankly I didn't want to outstay my welcome. Oliver Fairleigh was the sort of man who could have found some very unpleasant way of making that clear to one. He was very quick at registering boredom. We once dined him with a Bishop who'd done a book in our popular religious series, and Sir Oliver went to sleep during the main course. So I started to make time-to-go noises quite early, and he took me to the main door and saw me off down the steps. He could well have gone back to the study and had another glass or so after I'd gone.'

'True,' said Meredith. 'But come to that, we've no evidence of Mark Fairleigh-Stubbs going back to the house between that Sunday and the succeeding Saturday. It's all so damned nebulous.' He thought for a moment. 'Oh, and there was this business of *Black Widow*.'

'Er – Lady Fairleigh?' hazarded Mr Simmington vaguely.

'No. A book called *Black Widow*.' Getting no response but a polite expression of interest, mere bank-manager's courtesy, he went on: 'It was left to Lady Fairleigh in the will. I gather there is a book for posthumous publication, and I wondered – this is probably quite irrelevant to the case – whether this could be it.'

'You could well be right. No doubt it is. Miss Cozzens would be the one to ask. I've never been told the title.'

'Miss Cozzens says it was written before her time as secretary. She also says you probably have the manuscript here at Macpherson's.'

'No, no – I'm certain we don't have the manuscript.' By now the attitude of polite interest was being replaced by a very definite expression of alarm. 'You mean it's not at Wycherley Court? But this could be very serious. I can't tell you how annoyed Sir Edwin would be. He's – well, that's neither here nor there. But an Oliver Fairleigh book represents a very considerable amount of money to us. And the posthumous one – well, we were talking about it just before you came, as a matter of fact. It would naturally do even better than usual, and in view of the murder investigation – I don't have to spell that out for you, I'm sure, Inspector. Have you searched for it at Wycherley?'

'Miss Cozzens assures me it's not in her office, with all the proof copies and carbons. She suggested the study, and I went through it pretty thoroughly last evening. There's the rest of the house: I can put my men on to taking it apart.'

'Did you say it was written before Miss Cozzens's time? Yes, that would be right, I suppose. I heard about it when I joined the firm, which is more than seven years ago now. Things would have been different if Miss Cozzens had been responsible for the manuscript. I have the highest respect for her: her work is an editor's delight.'

'Did you know his previous secretary?'

'No, I've only been in charge of the Golden Dagger books for four years. My predecessor died – suicide, melancholia, between ourselves. But it's very likely there's someone here who would remember the name. Would you like me to ask around? And we could go through our files.'

'If you would. Of course, they will remember at Wycherley Court, but for the moment I prefer to have no one on their guard.'

'I see,' said Gerald Simmington. 'The question is, if he had *one* and not a succession. As you will have realized, it's not everyone could get along with Oliver Fairleigh.'

'No, indeed,' said Meredith, getting up and looking round for his mac. 'How did you manage?'

'I agreed with him all the time,' said Gerald Simmington, without a trace of a smile. 'And I made myself very inconspicuous, hardly worth noticing as a target.'

Meredith found it easy to believe. Mr Simmington seemed effortlessly to merge in with the wallpaper of his office (post-war austerity vintage). When he had led him through the labyrinth of dark corridors, shown him the main door, and shaken hands with him, Meredith looked at his retreating back, and found it difficult to remember what his face looked like.

At the street door he looked out on the June drizzle, and drew on his raincoat. He was not used to London. He realized he was not sure of his way back to the tube, and fished into his pocket for a street map, an aggravating aid that always got itself folded up in impossible ways. As he did so, the dragon-faced secretary from the outer office came out in a drab grey street coat, and Meredith asked her instead.

'Grreen Parrk,' she said, Edinburgh in her accent and her stance. 'I'll put you on your way.'

They walked down the dreadfully genteel little side street.

'It must be an interesting job you have, there,' hazarded Meredith.

'Very interesting,' she said, with an upward intonation. 'Especially the religious side.'

'Sir Edwin seemed an exceptionally easy person to work for,' went on Meredith. 'Very good-humoured.'

'Aye, he is,' volunteered the lady, looking ahead as if she disapproved of the question. 'Sir Edwin is a very pleasant man indeed. Your way lies there.' And nodding briskly, she took herself off in the other direction.

CHAPTER XII

SOMETHING UNSPOKEN

CHIEF INSPECTOR MEREDITH'S opinion of police boffins was that they were very clever indeed, but that criminals tended to be cleverer. Their methods sometimes seemed to border on the miraculous, and some of them clearly regarded themselves as the Cagliostros of our day, and yet the rate of crimes successfully solved by the police had not risen. This rather suggested that lots of people were one or two steps ahead of them.

By rights somebody's clothes should surely have contained traces of nicotine, if (for example) it had been carried in a phial and added to Sir Oliver's birthday lakka. But nobody's did. Meredith found that very interesting indeed, and a possible extension of the boffins' field of endeavour suggested itself to him. The trouble was, that their efforts were inevitably attended with a good deal of fuss: things had to be collected to be analysed, people were inevitably put on their guard. For the moment, he decided to keep the investigation as low key as possible: perhaps he might even be able to impress on the boffins (no, that was impossible, but to show them) how much could be achieved by the old-fashioned methods of foot-slogging, questioning and checking. He thanked his Methodist Lord however, that his rank put him beyond having to do any of this donkey-work himself.

'How are things in the house here?' he asked Sergeant Trapp, when he arrived back at Wycherley Court from London at lunch-time on Monday. 'Still one big happy family?'

'They're glowering,' said Sergeant Trapp, who had the longest ears in the business, and an insatiable relish for information gained by eavesdropping. 'One big long sulk, because Mark is very obviously in control. They're not taking it well at all. Could work to our advantage in the long run I suppose.'

'It could indeed. I propose, therefore, to leave them a little longer. You never know what tempests might brew up, and I suspect with Master Terence and Miss Bella in an acute state of disappointed expectations something or other is bound to. I think the time has come to look up the Woodstocks.'

'Fine old family,' murmured Sergeant Trapp, almost automatically, with an implied touch of the forelock.

'I've seen the boy around,' said Meredith iconoclastically. 'It looks as though the rot has set in.'

'He's got the family height, though,' said Trapp loyally. 'I remember his father, years ago it was, at the hunt meets and suchlike. He was a fine figure on a horse.'

'Do you think the Woodstocks resented the Fairleigh-Stubbs when they bought this place?'

'As interlopers? Could be, I suppose.' Trapp scratched his head. 'As far as I remember, they weren't in much of a position to resent them. By then they'd next to nothing themselves. And nobody could have resented Lady Fairleigh. She's their class, after all, or better.'

'Whereas Oliver Fairleigh – ?'

'Oh, he was in a class by himself,' said Trapp.

'Well, well,' said Meredith, tearing himself away from the delusive intricacies of the English class system in decay, 'I've a job for your lot. I want this house taken apart, in the gentlest possible way. I want to be sure this manuscript isn't here.'

'*Black Widow*?' Sergeant Trapp's eyebrows rose. 'Do you think it's worth the trouble?'

'How should I know till I find it? It may be. I'm sure it's worth while to keep a lot of people busy here. I'm pretty sure something nasty is going to blow up in the family. They might overhear it, and they might even be able to prevent something really nasty happening – something that would do none of our reputations any good.'

'So they're to search the house, and keep their ears open while they're about it, sir?'

'That's about it. Meanwhile I'm asking HQ for more men – ten more.'

'Whew. You'll be lucky. What for?'

'Oh, they'll give me them. If only because of all the stink this case is making.' He gestured vaguely in the direction of the front gate. 'Have you seen that lot out there? Journalistic cannibals, hungry for a bit of gristly flesh to be thrown in their direction. Until this case is solved, they'll be on our backs, and HQ will give us anything we ask for.'

He strode off to the study, having failed signally to answer the second part of Sergeant Trapp's question. However, when the same question was put to him by the Chief Commissioner, over the phone a couple of minutes later, he replied readily enough.

'I want a complete check on Mark Fairleigh-Stubbs's movements over the week before his father's death. Where he was, when, how long he stayed, who he talked to, who else was in the bar – when it's a question of bars, which I think it very largely will be. I want saturation coverage, every possible scrap of information they can give me.'

Having received assent, however grudging, and given all the necessary orders, Meredith strolled out of the house. The midday sun, in contrast to the drizzle of London, beat down on the official dark-blue metal of a police car on the tired lawns of Wycherley Court, and on the reporters at the gate, now swelled to a sweaty, gibbering crowd, looking and sounding like a cageful of monkeys performing frenetically for a solitary visitor. The thought of driving through that crowd was distasteful, as was the thought of them following him all the way to the Woodstock cottage and infesting the ground around it. A movement under a tree in the middle-distance caught his eye. He made out, in large floppy hat and heavy shoes, Lady Fairleigh, indulging in what must have been a long-standing panacea for domestic turmoil, gardening. He walked over towards her in as casual a way as possible.

'I wonder, is there any way of getting to the Wood-stocks' cottage without going through the main gate, Lady Fairleigh?' She looked startled, and he explained: 'I wanted to avoid those vampires over there.'

Her brow lost any sign of trepidation. 'Well, there is, of course,' she said, 'but it would mean a hike of twenty minutes or so.'

'Just what I need.'

'Then I'll show you the way.' They went together round to the back of the manor house. Meredith noticed what a strong, capable woman she looked, and how sturdily she walked. The nervous, fragile surface was no doubt a consequence of thirty years of marriage to Oliver Fairleigh, but the toughness that enabled her to stick it out was very visible under the surface. 'Tell me, Lady Fairleigh –' (again, that look!) – 'was there something odd about your husband's title?' The handsome, beaky face cleared again, and she looked at him almost roguishly.

'Well, not odd, exactly. A bit absurd, perhaps.'

'I'd always imagined he'd been knighted for his services to literature, or something.'

'Oh dear no. His books weren't good enough for that, surely? Though perhaps they ought to have given him something nice for staying in England and paying his taxes, and not nipping off to the Channel Islands or the Algarve as most of them do. No – the title is a baronetcy, and he inherited it in 1946.'

'Yes, I saw that in *The Times*. But why absurd?'

'Well, you know, his father bought it. Paid a mint of money for it, I believe, just before the fall of Lloyd George. The business wasn't going too well, and I think he thought the title would help – would give people confidence, and so on. But of course it didn't help at all. The world is full of bankrupt baronets.'

'I see. I suppose Sir Oliver preferred not to have this known?'

'Well, he preferred people not to talk about it. What was absurd, really, was that he valued the title so highly, when he and everyone knew how it had been obtained.'

'Did the older families in the district – ' they rounded a corner and made towards an overgrown corner of the estate – 'did the Woodstocks for example, rather resent your husband – an interloper, so to speak?'

'Oh, that sort of thing is rather out of date now, wouldn't you say, Inspector?' Lady Fairleigh looked at him quizzically. 'Like *Punch* cartoons of the 'twenties? Nowadays the people with money stick together, whatever their background. That's your way, Inspector, through that opening in the hedge. When you get to the lane, keep to your left and it's about a mile.'

'But the Woodstocks, Lady Fairleigh,' said Meredith, putting a hand on her arm to detain her, 'have family but *no* money.'

'In that sort of case, Inspector, the people with money are . . . kind.'

'I see. Would you say it was to maintain the family position in the area that your husband left the whole of his estate, virtually intact, to his elder son?'

An expression passed over her face which he interpreted as distaste for talking about family affairs with a stranger. But her sturdy common sense soon showed her the absurdity of the feeling. She said: 'Yes, I would, on thinking about it. I genuinely never knew what Oliver had put in the will, you know – never asked. But in retrospect it seems the obvious thing, the thing he *would* do. Oliver knew that even if the first generation was a bit of an interloper, the second would be "old-established." And he would want the title and the money to go together. He never valued one without the other.'

'Hard on the younger children, perhaps?'

'Perhaps. Or perhaps better for them in the long run. A *little* money, extra pocket money so to speak, can be nice. But a little *more*, nearly enough but not quite enough to live on without working – that can be ruinous, don't you think? They'll have to get over the disappointment. And I *do* think Mark is behaving well . . . ?' She looked at him, almost appealingly, as if hoping he would agree with her. Against his better judgement he responded.

'He's being very responsible indeed.'

She breathed a sigh of thanks. 'There was never any hope of our being a *happy* family, Inspector. I've never had any ambitions beyond keeping the peace. I still hope to be able to do that.'

This time he could not keep her, and he watched her potter off across the gardens, looking here and there at shrubs and flowers for signs that they were doing well. Gardens were so much more hopeful than families.

The Woodstock cottage affected Meredith much as it had done Oliver Fairleigh. The bright colours it had been painted, the arrangement of the newly-dug flower-beds, the looped-up curtains, all somehow seemed intolerably twee. It looked like the sort of place where one would be offered dandelion tea. Here he did Celia Woodstock an injustice. She offered him perfectly ordinary tea, with the alternative of parsnip wine.

The Woodstocks were very friendly, and terribly relaxed.

'You know, it's a bit of a thrill, this, Inspector,' said Ben, curving his etiolated length around the fireplace and stuffing his bony fingers into his pipe. 'You probably know I write detective stories too. It's an incredibly lucky thing to have experience of a real police investigation, and I feel I'm testing my powers of observation too.'

Inspector Meredith, sinking into the armchair and into the overwhelmingly cosy atmosphere, brought down the shutters across his dancing eyes, but kept them surreptitiously on Ben. A gaunt face, seemingly almost concave, with deep dark sockets for eyes and hair brought deliberately down slant-wise across his forehead. A Hamlet face, but totally without magnetism. Sitting there, Meredith felt himself bursting with life in comparison with both the Woodstocks, for somehow there hung about both of them this odd, enervated air, this feeling of predestined mediocrity and failure. And yet, Ben had had the nerve to strike out on his own, to forgo the delusive securities of regular wage-packet and pension scheme and write full time. As sometimes happened, what the man did, and the impression the man gave, simply did not come together to make a whole. He didn't gel.

'The trouble is,' said Meredith, conversationally taking up Woodstock's last point, 'that of course nobody *knows* this sort of thing is going to happen, and often they notice very little.'

'But I feel, you know, that as a writer I *should* be observant, be on the watch the whole time.'

'Ben has almost total recall,' said his wife proudly, coming in with a tray of china and a teapot, and settling herself down as the completing item in the picture of domesticity around the hearth. 'Of course, it's a terribly unnerving gift to have at times, but in a case like this it couldn't be more useful!'

'Very true!' said Meredith, unhooding his eyelids and casting in her direction a glance of dutiful gallantry. She gave a nervous little giggle as she fussed over the tea things. She was a dumpy little body, without any style but with limitless surface good-will. He had known girls who seemed to be nature's wives and mothers yet turned out on closer acquaintance to be monsters of ambition and greed, Catherine the Greats of hearth and home. He accepted his cup, and sank back in his chair, letting them dictate the atmosphere.

'I hope this will meet with your approval, Inspector,' said Ben, producing a rough manuscript. 'I've written out an account of last Saturday evening. I did it, really, as a sort of test for myself, to try to bring back absolutely everything I noticed and could remember. I hope it might be useful to you. I haven't tried to select at all, just put in everything.'

'That sounds like a policeman's ideal sort of testimony.'

'I thought that as outsiders we were in a particularly good position to see things that other people may have missed.'

'Coming quite fresh to it,' said Celia, 'and not really knowing the people concerned.'

'Exactly,' said Meredith, in his friendly way. 'A completely unbiased account is just what I need.'

'Now, I've been assuming, Inspector,' said Ben, uncurling himself from the mantelpiece and draping himself across the chair opposite, 'that his drink – the Finnish stuff, whatever it was called – was poisoned. Of course, I'm not pumping you – I just wanted to explain why I've gone into a lot of detail just at that point in the narrative, detail about positions around the desk in the study, and so on.'

'That will be particularly useful,' said Meredith, which was true, if the accuracy of the account could be confirmed.

'Of course, dinner was difficult, with lots of conversations going on at the same time. But I've written out what I remembered, and Celia has done the same.'

'It's a very *plain* account,' said Celia Woodstock, as if apologizing for her lack of the literary graces. 'I just put down what I could remember, and tried to get it in the right order. Anyway, if it's any help, there it is.' She smiled brightly. The helpfulness of the Woodstocks was overwhelming.

'You've gone to a lot of trouble,' said Meredith.

'Not at all, Inspector,' said Ben. 'As I say, I regarded it as a most interesting exercise. Also – '

'Yes?'

'Well, I have to admit, there has been an offer from one of the Sunday newspapers. I don't know, it's terrible to capitalize on the Fairleighs' troubles like this, but of course it *is* a chance to get my name known, and if I could manage to do something tasteful and inoffensive . . .'

You'll find they have ways to turn it into something tasteless and offensive, thought Meredith to himself. But he said: 'Of course, I can see you wouldn't want to offend the Fairleighs. You are old friends, aren't you?'

'Hardly that, Inspector,' said Celia briskly. 'I hadn't met any of them apart from Lady Fairleigh until ten days ago.'

'It was really one of those casual acquaintanceships on my part,' said Ben, stretching his long, runner-bean legs out from the chair with an invincibly casual air. 'I used to go and play tennis now and then during the summer. I think I once went to a birthday party, I forget whose. I had completely lost touch with them, until Sir Oliver and Lady Fairleigh came here to lunch last Sunday.'

'Did you find them changed?'

'Changed? Oh no. They never changed. I remember Sir Oliver on my visits as a boy. Terrifying. He'd join in our games, when he was in a good mood, and cheat outrageously: he'd be daring us to challenge him, staring at us with those great bulging eyes. Or he'd come and watch the tennis and start shouting things like a Liverpool hooligan at a football match – screaming crazy abuse and accusing us of fouls, and so on. Then at meal times he'd boom unanswerable questions at you, or conduct ridiculous inquisitions: "Who's your favourite author?"

"George Eliot, sir." "Who's he? Never heard of him. Explain who he is." "It's a woman, sir – " And so on, until eventually he would be maintaining that she was a disguised criminal in hiding from the police, or a music hall artist specializing in drag. It's quite funny in retrospect, but it was awful at the time.'

'There are ways of doing things like that,' agreed Meredith.

'Exactly,' said Ben. 'And of course he wasn't trying to amuse us, but to amuse himself.'

'As I said on the way there, Inspector,' said Celia primly, 'it's not a family I'd want to have *much* to do with.'

'Of course, basically the poor old chap was bored,' said Ben tolerantly. 'Anything to inject a spark of life into the proceedings. I tell you, I thought he was having us on for a moment last Saturday when he collapsed. I thought he'd suddenly get up, all red and outraged, and go on with the party.'

It occurred to Meredith that Woodstock was coming to life, and that the reason was not so much that he was enjoying being a vital witness in a police investigation, but that he was rehearsing a lucrative article for the *Sunday Grub*. The picture was vivid enough for him not to want to complain, but it did make him suspect that Ben's relationship with the Fairleighs must have gone a lot deeper than he tried to pretend.

'So you and the family haven't really kept up the acquaintanceship in the years since then?' he asked.

'No,' said Ben, switching back to his casual depreciative pose. 'Of course, I've been at Cambridge, and then I did some British Council work abroad. And the three over there have been – well, all over the place. I imagine Saturday night's get-together was a pretty rare thing for the Fairleighs. No, I'm afraid we'd all drifted apart. You know how it is. My mother and Lady Fairleigh visit, and telephone now and again. Nothing more than that.'

'Isn't Bella Fairleigh a writer too, in a way – ?'

'A journalist, Inspector. Quite a different kettle of fish,

if that doesn't sound too snobbish.' Ben Woodstock's face creased into a smile, which wasn't much of a smile. 'Except of course that that's what I intend to be for the next few days, if I can establish a really tight contract.'

Meredith felt that Ben Woodstock had ignored the implication of his question, and slithered rather neatly towards another subject. He rather thought that Celia Woodstock (who he suspected was not quite the cabbage she looked) had also noticed, and had tensed up. She was, though, in her prim, conventional way, a rather resourceful girl, and as Meredith began to make getting-up movements, it was she who spoke.

'I *do* hope things are not too terrible over at Wycherley Court. They must be *dreadfully* worried and unhappy. Are they facing up to it well?'

'Very well,' said Meredith, all blandness. 'Sir Mark has taken over, and he's proving a tower of strength.'

He caught their reactions as he eased himself up from the chair. Ben's eyebrows shot up, and he asked involuntarily: 'Mark? Then it's Mark who – ? But of course we mustn't ask.'

The implications of his remark had not been lost on Celia Woodstock either. Her face, for one moment, was a picture of triumphant spite. Then they both cosily showed him to the door.

Reading at leisure, in the cool of the early evening, the accounts by Ben and Celia Woodstock of their evening at Wycherley Court, Meredith was struck by two contrary impressions.

On the one hand Ben had, as he said, been enormously detailed. His account resembled nothing so much as one of those semi-documentary novels which piles trivial fact upon trivial fact in an effort to demonstrate that fiction can (with a bit of effort) be twice as boring as life. Just as the authors of these will spare one nothing, from the position of the fillings in the hero's teeth to the name of the second housemaid's brother-in-law, so Ben threw in the kitchen sink and left him to do the selecting. His account of positions around the desk during the opening of the presents was admirable. The drinks cabinet was slightly to the left of the desk, on the wall; Ben made it clear that positions changed during the unwrapping of the various gifts, so that he, Celia, Terry and Bella had all been close to the decanter of lakka at one time or another. Lady Fairleigh had, on the other hand, remained close to the coffee table on the right. All this was excellent and (subject to checking) useful. Ben was also quite specific on the subject of Mark: he was, he felt sure, quite drunk. He did not get up, and could not have got up, from his chair at the far end of the study, the whole time the Woodstocks were there, which was until a few minutes after Oliver Fairleigh had been taken off in the ambulance.

On the other hand, the suspicious mind might well wonder if there had not been omissions in the Woodstocks' accounts. Celia mentioned Oliver Fairleigh's affability and volubility, yet apparently they had talked about nothing but some people she knew slightly from Birmingham who were also acquaintances of Sir Oliver, and of the prospect of his inviting Ben to lunch with Sir Edwin Macpherson. It seemed a meagre haul for a conversation that spanned sherry and four whole courses.

Ben, on the other hand, gave an apparently full account of his conversation with Bella – journalism, London literary life, friends in common – but his version was totally lacking in life and verve. It read like the conversation of two pensioners who had met casually on a park bench. The account given by Surtees of their behaviour at table had given a very different impression.

Meredith wondered whether, by giving a minute description of the bark and foliage of the trees, Ben Woodstock had not been trying to conceal the wood. At any rate, it seemed safer to regard his recall as selective rather than total.

### CHAPTER XIII

## DE MORTUIS ...

IT WAS TUESDAY before the newspapers really got into their stride over the Oliver Fairleigh murder. Monday's edition had given him plenty of space, with zoom-lens pictures of his son at the door of his newly-inherited stately home. On Tuesday the police announcement that they were treating the case as one of murder removed all inhibitions, except the purely legal ones. It was clear that the jabbering mass of journalists at the gate of Wycherley Court was but a small portion of the sum total of industry and talent being devoted to the story. Oliver Fairleigh's death, and therefore by extension his life, was for the moment the hottest news story in the country.

Fleet Street has never set great store by the maxim that only good should be spoken of the dead. On this occasion, however, it could afford to let the deceased speak ill of himself. Oliver Fairleigh had been a prolific contributor to all but the most reputable organs of opinion: through his articles he found he could (within certain limits which he was careful to observe) attack, injure and insult people, races, institutions and habits of which he disapproved, and earn quite disproportionate sums for doing so. Now he was dead, the newspapers reprinted long extracts from the articles on which they held the copyright, and the collected crassness, wrong-headedness and spleen made the man infinitely more petty and ridiculous than any character assassination by a third party could.

His political pronouncements were perhaps oddest of all. Over the years a political event was judged solely by the criteria of whether it confirmed his dire prophecies or conformed to his deepest prejudices; if it did, it was greeted with a shriek of delight. The troubles in Ireland and the State of Emergency in India were sources of the purest pleasure for him, supporting as they did his firm conviction that both peoples were incapable of governing themselves. The Conservative Party kept a vestigial hold on his allegiance as long as it was arguably an aristocratic party, but the advent of Mr Heath was met with howls of anguish ('the apotheosis of the board-school boy'), and the reign of his successor led to a vitriolic article on the subject of women in politics, a series of savage sketches of the careers of the two Señoras Peron, Mrs Meir, Mrs Gandhi and Mrs Bandaranaike, leading up to a detailed but not too convincing comparison between Mrs Thatcher and Catherine the Great.

For the rest, his articles were hysterical swipes in all directions, particularly at every manifestation of the modern world that came under his beady-eyed notice. Teddy boys, Aldermaston-marchers, hippies, pop groups, druggies, skin-heads, all had in their turn been greeted with hymns of hate. However, while his viewpoint on his subject was very often likely to be identical with that of the readers he was aiming at, he almost always conducted his attack in such a way as to alienate most of the very people he might be supposed to be appealing to. It seemed to Meredith, reading through the depressing collection in the writer's own study, early on Tuesday morning, as if the sole purpose had been to offend as many people as possible simultaneously. A description of Scottish Nationalism which had Meredith mildly chuckling would be followed by a description of the Welsh people that brought a hot flush to his face, and set those eyes sparkling dangerously.

But it was all too random to carry conviction. 'It is sometimes suggested,' began one piece, 'that as a nation we care too much about cruelty to animals, and not enough about cruelty to children. I do not, myself, see this as an "either/or" situation: personally I care about both of them, and get quite as much pleasure from the one

as from the other.' Ho-ho, thought the reader: Oliver
Fairleigh trying to be clever.

The newspapers covered very fully all his more public
escapades, from his attempt to enter Parliament ('Madam,'
he was reported to have told a heckling housewife, 'if I
allowed my opinions to be influenced by an ignorant
harridan like you, I would consider myself unfit to
represent this constituency at Westminster') to his
relationship with his elder son (his notice in *The Times*
disclaiming responsibility for his debts was one of the few
occasions in his career when he enjoyed universal sympathy for his point of view, nobody in Fleet Street,
apparently, having paused to wonder whether a young
man brought up by Oliver Fairleigh might not have had
in the course of his childhood things to put up with which
could justify a modicum of wildness or irresponsibility).

What was lacking was the usual pen-portrait by a
friend. The reason for this, Meredith guessed, was simple
enough: for the last thirty years Oliver Fairleigh had had
none. There was a reminiscence of him in the 'thirties by
another member of the Auden-Isherwood group, an
obscure figure long since sunk into the grooves of academe.
The piece lacked impact, perhaps because Oliver Fairleigh was himself at that time a mass of unformed clay,
waiting to be moulded to the protuberant shape of his
maturity, and coloured with the bright red of outrage.

The nearest any piece came to intimacy was one by
someone called the Hon. Darcy Howard, whom the
newspapers called 'poet and man of letters,' and described
as the dead man's cousin. Putting two and two together,
Meredith decided the description must be wrong: he was
Lady Fairleigh's uncle. Reading the article, he decided
that the 'poet and man of letters' bit was beside the mark
too. It was a slack, rambling piece, without style or shape.
It chronicled the author's acquaintanceship with the
young Oliver Fairleigh in the seedier salons of literary
London both before and just after the war. It described
hilarious adventures, not particularly either, in Italy in

nineteen forty-three and four, when Oliver Fairleigh was with and Darcy Howard 'attached to' the Allied Forces. It described the meeting of Fairleigh and the author's niece, and the marriage. Subsequent meetings between the author and his subject had apparently been few, or unmemorable.

The article was illustrated by two photographs. One was of Darcy Howard himself, standing at the gate of a rather run-down cottage in Wiltshire, his home. It had clearly been taken the day before, probably while he took a breather from penning his reminiscences: he was a man in his seventies, sadly seedy, with a slack mouth and watery, disreputable eyes. The other was a snapshot from Italy, depicting Darcy Howard, Oliver Fairleigh and a conventionally pretty ATS private, arms around each others' shoulders, with a Sicilian piazza in the background. Oliver Fairleigh – tubby then, rather than corpulent – was in uniform, but both men were somewhat dishevelled and were brandishing fiaschi of wine, smiling broadly. The younger, gayer Oliver Fairleigh was like a distant ancestor of the Fairleigh the world knew, a figure related but totally unlike: it was a personality which had passed without trace, trampled under by the passing years. The caption under the trio, frozen in their moment of jollity, read simply: 'Second-lieutenant Fairleigh, with friends.'

All in all, the quality of the reminiscences on that Tuesday was pretty low, but the *Daily Grub* announced that its sister Sunday paper would be running a sensational account of the last dinner by the up-and-coming young novelist Ben Woodstock, who was present at the death. Their regular readers would have to control their impatience, to give Ben time to polish his phrases.

It was nearly ten o'clock in the morning, but Eleanor Fairleigh was still in bed, asleep. She had been fretfully tossing and turning until the early hours, and then had fallen off. Now, deep in a dreamy sleep, she was living her life without Oliver Fairleigh, and without her children.

She was alone, and all there was to disturb her was a nagging voice at the back of her brain that said: 'But this is Death!'

Downstairs, her children were at breakfast, quarrelling.

The quarrel had begun spasmodically, for Bella and Terence were at a disadvantage, and had been since their father's death. Normally in such circumstances a rich store of possible grievances has been laid by, to launch at the head of the unlucky heir: he has fawned on the dead, he has ingratiated himself in an unprincipled way, he has misused his position. None of these time-honoured missiles could in the present case be used. Mark had barely spoken to his father over the last few years other than to abuse or quarrel with him. Yet here he sat, at the head of the breakfast table, calmly chomping his way through a substantial meal and doubtless contemplating a future of well-heeled leisure. From being the black sheep he had been transformed overnight into the fat cat, enjoying the cream. In the circumstances there was little to be done except vent spite, in however random a manner.

'I envy you your appetite,' said Bella bitterly, pushing aside her crust of toast.

'Do you, Bella?' said Mark, continuing to eat. 'I'm sorry if it annoys you in any way. But I think it would annoy you still more if I pretended that grief had robbed me of my appetite.'

He put a forkful of devilled kidney into his mouth. His hand was not quite steady, and that unformed, handsome face showed signs of strain – though not the usual strain of an acute hangover. Perhaps if either of the others had encouraged him to take a drink at that moment, he would have found it hard to resist. But both of them were too self-absorbed to notice any strain in him. And, in any case, why encourage him now to make a fool of himself? Now it was pointless.

'You've got nothing to put you off your appetite,' said Terence, gazing savagely at his plate.

'Nor have you, dear brother, if you thought about it,'

said Mark, annoyingly smooth. 'You've been living in a silly dream, and you've been woken up.'

'If he'd lived,' said Bella, her voice gaining again that harsh, harridan quality, 'he would have left it to me.'

'It's just possible,' said Mark, finishing off his plateful of food, and leaning back in his chair with a cup of coffee. 'Though I must say it seems to me far from probable. But I admit your case is a little different from Terence's. He is sore at losing something he never had a chance of getting. You can convince yourself that it was only through bad luck and lack of time that you lost out. Quite apart from any grief you may feel at the loss of Father.'

'I *am* sorry he's dead. I *did* love him,' said Bella.

'Perhaps. I doubt whether you can sort your emotions out sufficiently to tell. I find it difficult enough.'

'The question is,' said Terence, raising his Shelleyan fair head with the bloodshot eyes, 'what are you going to do for us?'

It was the question both of them had been wanting to ask, but as he let it out, baldly, because there seemed no point in trying to wrap it up for Mark, both Terence and Bella felt the treacherousness of the ground. Mark leaned forward, took a piece of toast, and spread it with butter in an infuriatingly leisurely manner.

'I find that difficult to answer,' he said. 'Of course, you will admit that I owe you nothing.'

'You owe us plenty,' said Bella, her voice rising. 'You got everything, we got nothing.'

'Yes. In normal circumstances, I suppose I might feel some sort of moral debt,' said Mark, busy with the marmalade. 'In fact, I can imagine myself shelling out quite heroically to salve my conscience. But you know, in the actual circumstances, I don't. Not at all.'

There was silence in the room. Mark ate on contentedly, and looked round at the other two. It was they who had started the subject, he seemed to say, let them continue it if they wanted to. The silence eventually became unbearable, and Bella had to ask: 'What circumstances?'

In the pause which Mark left before replying, Surtees came in with a fresh pot of coffee, and began clearing away plates. Mark said: '*Circonstances que tu connais bien, Bella.*'

'*C'est pas nécessaire à parler français,*' hissed Bella.

'Why not?' said Mark, continuing to. 'Is he the sort of lover you have no secrets from, Bella?'

Surtees continued round the table, impassively gathering up plates and serving dishes. He gave no sign of having understood, but as he finished what he was doing, and walked carefully towards the door with his tray, he blinked twice, as if absorbing new developments, and when he went out he failed to shut the door properly behind him. Perhaps Mark, with his preparatory and public school education, did not appreciate how widely French has become taught in State schools. Surtees went down to the kitchen, and swore at Mrs Moxon when she tried to pump him about what was being said in the breakfast-room.

Meanwhile, in the hall, Sergeant Trapp, seeing the door to the breakfast-room swing very slightly open, tiptoed with surprising delicacy over to it, and stationed himself nonchalantly outside. The conversation inside had, luckily, reverted to English.

'Do you know what happens, Bella, when you suddenly stop drinking?' Mark was saying, leaning forward across the table and speaking with a low, passionate intensity. 'I'll tell you. First of all it feels like the world has fallen on top of you. Then after a bit, you blink and look around you, like a horse coming out of its stables in the morning, and you start seeing things as they are. But it's not just that, because you've got a lot of memories – very hazy ones, just wisps here and there. They start coming back, one by one – a little thing here, a little thing there – things you didn't know you'd noticed. Things other people didn't think you would notice, because you were blind drunk. And these things start falling into place.'

'And – ?' asked Bella, struggling to regain her usual pose

of utter coolness.

'And – you come to various conclusions about what's been going on while you've been stuck out there on your little alcoholic cloud. Just to take a little example: I realize that you've been using Surtees – the faithful servant, Crichton *de nos jours* – to go along to Father with every little bit of gossip and dirt he can pick up about me. I suspect, by the way, that you needn't have bothered, because I guess Father paid him for doing exactly the same service. But anyway, you have paid him by sleeping with him, without any particular reluctance, I should guess.'

'Evidence?' spat out Bella.

'None, sister dear. I'm not a policeman. I don't need to have everything cast-iron. The odd bit of gossip in a pub; your name and a snigger – because Surtees talks in his cups too, I suspect. Then the fact that he very much wants to stay on, and I can't quite believe it's out of loyalty to me, or the ancestral name. These things are nothing – hardly even straws in the wind. But they convince me, and really, I'm afraid, that's all that matters.'

'You're despicable, Mark,' said Bella, leaning back in her chair and lighting up a cigarette, and seeming in an odd way relieved. 'You're clutching on to fantastic excuses, so as not to do anything for us, and that's all there is to it.'

'Quite,' said Mark. 'I knew you'd say that. And that's what you can tell everybody, too, when you spread your hard-luck story. I've cultivated a very thick skin about what people say about me over the last few years, and I think it's going to stand me in very good stead.'

He poured himself a large cup of coffee from the new pot. He had relaxed since the moment of intensity earlier, but he gave the impression of being a man preparing himself for another spring.

'Actually,' he said casually, 'as far as you're concerned, Bella, I'm willing to be charitable.' Involuntarily she turned towards him. 'I'm willing to assume that you knew nothing of Brother Terence's plan.'

'Ah,' said Terence, with a Mick Jagger sneer, but his voice not quite steady, 'what are we going to bring up from the lucky dip this time? More hazy fantasies from the seven years' blind?'

'Quite recent ones, these,' said Mark. 'I think you've only recently started thinking about money and inheritances and the like. But when you start, you work quickly, don't you, Terry? It's convenient not to have any awkward, old-fashioned things like scruples or compunctions, isn't it? It enables you to go straight to the guts of the matter, doesn't it, and really get down to the job.'

'Taking up evangelical religion, Mark?' asked Terence coolly. 'Come on, skip the New Testament asides. What have you dredged up out of your dream world for me?'

Again Mark leaned forward: 'I think that you never really knew what Father was likely to do with his money, never having in your life thought about anyone but yourself for more than half a second at a time. But you had this nagging suspicion at the back of your mind, that *perhaps* Father wouldn't want to cut me off, that *perhaps* he'd want the money and the title to go together.'

'So?'

'So you thought: if he *is* in the will after all these years and everything he's done, then it's going to need something really serious to get him out. There's been debts, and drunkenness, and rudeness, so what does it take? And you thought that something not just on the windy side of the law, but something really criminal, with a big scandal and prison at the end of it, might do the trick.'

'I see,' said Terence, looking straight back into his brother's brown eyes. 'And what did I plan to do: leave you in the vaults of the Bank of England while you were dead drunk?'

'It's odd, but in the past month I've had three offers to go into the drug trade. Odd coincidence, isn't it? Tempt-

ing offers, they were. I was to be a middle-man, a dis-
tributor. They knew – whoever "they" were, Terence –
that I went around the country, and that no one would be
surprised if I turned up in this pub or that one. They
made it sound very simple and nice: it was just a question
of arranging meetings with people, passing the stuff over
in lavatories, and so on. Nothing dirty about the trade at
all, the way they told it. And it was very tempting, in
view of the sums involved. It would have been so easy to
say yes.'

'I'm surprised you didn't,' said Terence. 'Which is a
fair enough indication that it never happened.'

'Well, you don't want me to preach, so I won't tell you
all the reasons why I didn't, but the fact is, there was also
a bad bit of carelessness on your part, little brother. One
of the men who made me an offer seemed just a bit
familiar. I couldn't put a name to him, but I knew I'd
seen him somewhere. I went into your bedroom the other
day, and looked at that poster of your group. He's your
bass guitarist. Some bad planning on your part there,
Terry.'

'It's crap,' said Terence, looking at him viciously, his
red lips pursed. 'You're living in a fantasy world.'

'So now you see,' said Mark, now quite relaxed and
totally in command, 'why I feel no obligations. If you ever
get anything, either of you – and it won't be much – it
will be charity, pure charity, without an ounce of moral
obligation on my part. And of course there is one other
thing, one other possibility. I'm trying to put that from
my mind, but at the moment I'm not entirely succeeding.
Do you know what would happen if I went down to the
Wycherley Arms tonight for a pint?' The other two
frowned, not seeing what he was driving at. 'The landlord
would serve me quickly, and make sure he had business in
the other bar. And everyone would edge away and drink
up in a hurry. And all because last Sunday I said my
father ought to be shot, and a week later he was dead.'

Mark put his napkin aside and pushed his chair back. The others watched him, resentment written across their faces like a neon sign.

'Of course, people jump to conclusions,' he went on. 'But the possibility remains that someone heard about what I'd said, and tried to make a very nasty use of it. It was a very fair bet that the police would jump to the conclusion that I'd threatened my father, and then done what I threatened. It was a nice little notion, and but for the grace of alcohol it would probably have succeeded.' He got up, and leaned on the back of his chair. 'But still, it didn't succeed. And whoever had the idea has failed, and can't make it succeed now. And before long, I *shall* be able to go into the Wycherley Arms. And they'll call me "Sir Mark" there, and I'll buy drinks all round. And then I'll walk home to this house, and I'll go round from room to room – yours will have to be redecorated, Terry – and I'll sit down in the study, and have a cigar, and I'll say to myself: "This is all mine. And it came to me without my ever cringing, or flattering, or doing anybody down. I have no debts to the past." And I shall sleep – very, very well.'

He walked out of the breakfast-room, across the hall (where Sergeant Trapp was over by the front door, contemplating the June morning) and into the drawing-room, where he sat in an armchair and brooded long and gloomily over the morning papers.

At his feet, Cuff slept, noisily. It was almost like the old days again, he thought.

### CHAPTER XIV

## Downstairs, Upstairs

Sergeant trapp's narration of the conversation at the breakfast table – Meredith blessed for the thousandth time that miraculous combination of sharp ears and accurate memory – was interrupted by a call from Gerald Simmington at Macpherson's.

'No news of the missing manuscript yet?' he asked, his grey voice sounding almost urgent.

'Afraid not, sir, not yet,' said Meredith. 'We've taken the whole house apart, and the only result is that we're pretty sure it's not here now. The only thing is to hope for is that when the case is solved, the question of the whereabouts of *Black Widow* will become clear at the same time.'

'I fervently hope so,' said Mr Simmington. From his tone it might have been gathered that the loss of *Black Widow* was comparable to that of Byron's Memoirs or Emily Brontë's second novel, or at any rate that it would be counted so at Macpherson's. He explained. 'Sir Edwin is most put out. If it has disappeared, it will represent a considerable loss to us.'

Inspector Meredith didn't quite like the word 'loss' to describe something they had never had, but he merely said: 'To change the subject just slightly, have you had any luck with the question of the last secretary?'

'Well, a little. Not enough, perhaps. She left about seven years ago, some months before Miss Cozzens was engaged. There may have been some temporary help in between, because Sir Oliver was careful before engaging anyone permanently. There's been a period when he had five or six in a row, none of them staying more than a few weeks, so he had to make sure he got someone who could stand him.' Mr Simmington seemed to feel he had put too much emotion into the last words, and amended them to 'could put up with his little ways. Anyway, the previous one left in a cloud – or at any rate, there was some kind of row. Nobody remembers what, or probably ever knew, here.'

'And nobody knows where she went?'

'Well, the general impression seems to be that she retired. She was certainly old, and people have the idea that the row, or whatever it was, only hastened things by a few months.'

'I suppose nobody remembers her name?'

Mr Simmington's voice seemed to take on a tut-tut of disapproval at the lack of method in the ways of lesser human beings: 'Everybody does, but it's not quite the same name. Unfortunately we toothcombed our files a couple of years ago, and there's no note of hers left here. There are lots of suggestions from the older members of staff, all vaguely similar. Fennington seems the most likely, Fuddleston the least. It must be something along those lines.'

'Well then, I'll have to ask the family. I've been trying so far to keep them fairly in the dark about what I'm after, but there'll have to be some kind of confrontation before very long. Tell Sir Edwin I'm keeping the manuscript very much in mind.'

'I'll do that, Inspector.' Once more Mr Simmington's voice was that of the faithful office spaniel. 'He'll be *very* glad to hear it.'

Meredith put down the phone, and turned his mind back to Sergeant Trapp's recital. Since he had been posted outside the door, he was unable to embellish the conversation with descriptions of facial expressions, but Sergeant Trapp was useful precisely for the fact that he did not go in for embellishment. He recounted, and where possible reproduced the intonation of, the conversation over breakfast, and enjoyed himself hugely. At the end of it, as Trapp drew himself up to full height in self-satisfaction, Meredith said: 'Really one big happy family, aren't they? I suppose with a father like that, one couldn't hope for anything better.'

'I don't believe in blaming the parents always,' said Sergeant Trapp, who had a son in modelling.

'You believe in original sin, eh? Well, as a Welshman, I won't go against that. On the whole it's a much more simple and satisfying explanation, I grant you that.'

'Either way, they're a pretty nasty bunch. I thought it opened up all sorts of possibilities, what Sir Mark said.'

'Oh, you're right. And it closes down some as well.' Seeing Sergeant Trapp look disappointed and bewildered, Meredith went on: 'When all the reports are in about Mark Fairleigh's activities over the past week, we'll do a bit of checking on that bass guitarist. Meanwhile, I think I'll take a look downstairs – in the servants' quarters, or whatever one calls them these days: "the domestic operatives' enclave," I suppose.'

'I don't like the look of that Surtees,' said Trapp.

'Well, if you don't, there's probably plenty that do,' said Meredith. 'Including, I'm quite sure, the man himself. I've never felt such a glow of invincible self-admiration from anyone in my life before. Keep those ears at it, my boy.'

And he trotted off, through the baize door and down the wide stone stairs to the enormous, almost luxurious kitchen: it had been extensively modernized, no doubt to keep Mrs Moxon happy, and there was about it an air both of infinite room and of comfort. Meredith had turned up most opportunely. Mid-morning coffee was in progress, and it looked as if it was serving as a sort of servants' council. Round the table were seated Surtees, Mrs Moxon, whom Meredith had briefly glimpsed some days before, Wiggens the gardener, and – somewhat apart, and sitting much more upright and angular – Miss Cozzens.

'Well,' said Mrs Moxon, slapping down her cup on her saucer as she observed his approach down the stairs, 'about time I'd say.' She folded her arms across her ballooning bosom, and prepared to be a vital witness. Miss Cozzens, on the other hand, perhaps not quite happy at being caught fraternizing, prepared to slip away.

'Oh, before you go, Miss Cozzens – '

'Yes, Inspector?' There was reluctance in the set of her hips, in the swing of her sensible navy skirt.

'Did you check on the methods of killing Sir Oliver used in his various books, as you said you would?'

'Yes, I did. He never used nicotine poisoning at all. Of the poisonings he used arsenic twice, cyanide once and strychnine once. Not very many, but as I said, it wasn't his favourite method of killing. There was one with arsenic in the toad-in-the-hole. It's one of the Mrs Merrydale ones, where she uses her domestic instincts to solve the mystery. But it's not very like, is it? In fact, none of the killings was anything like Sir Oliver's death, with the poisoned drink, the toasts and so on. I have all the various references upstairs, should you need them, Inspector.'

'That's very thorough of you, Miss Cozzens. But I don't expect to have to bother you. It looks as though, at least until we find *Black Widow*, we won't find anything very close to the way Oliver Fairleigh died.'

'You've found no trace of it, then?'

'None at all. Sir Edwin Macpherson is very concerned.'

'Well, he would be, wouldn't he?'

'For money reasons, you mean?'

'Well, it's certainly not the loss to literature that bothers him.' Miss Cozzens slapped her mouth to, in her not very humorous smile. 'He will have to make do with *Murder Upstairs and Downstairs*. The case will still be fresh in everybody's mind when it comes out in October. Sir Edwin will be coining money from it.'

'He has the manuscript to that, of course.'

'Oh yes. We were so behind with it I clean-typed most of it before it was quite finished – not a thing I would normally do, in case of changes. Sir Oliver came and got them after dinner when Mr Simmington was here, and handed them over himself. He settled down to get the last chapters done the next day, and finished them in a morning. He could always get down to work if he wanted to. He would have hated to miss the Christmas market.'

Receiving a polite nod of thanks from Meredith, Barbara Cozzens fixed her mouth into a thin, prim line, and walked purposefully away. The whole set of her body told Meredith she had not liked being questioned in front of the servants. In the elaborate dance of social do's and don't's, he seemed to have trodden on her toe.

The other three, meanwhile, had been following the conversation with eager half-comprehension, and – in the case of Mrs Moxon – with some twitches of irritation. Policemen who came down to her kitchen should concentrate their attention on her. She had twice folded her arms over her matronly bosom, in passable imitation of Mrs Bridges, and when Miss Cozzens went up the stairs, she did it again. Mrs Moxon, it seemed, was determined to be, not just Mrs Moxon, but 'Cook'.

'Right,' she pronounced finally. 'And as I said a moment ago, not before time. Now, what do you want to know?'

'Lovely to find you so co-operative, ma'am,' said Meredith, imperceptibly exaggerating his Welsh singsong. 'I've been looking forward to a little chat, like. Saving you up, you might say. We needn't trouble you, Mr Surtees,' he went on, turning towards him, 'since we've been over things, you and I.'

'No trouble,' said Surtees, sitting on massively, his face a mixture of curiosity and conceit. Meredith, his whole manner changing suddenly, fixed him with an eye of steely determination, and said nothing. Eventually Surtees grudgingly shifted his bulk, and let himself out of the door into the garden.

'Good riddance to bad rubbish,' said Mrs Moxon. 'The less you have to do with that type, the better.' This was ungrateful of Mrs Moxon, for as a matter of fact she normally had a high opinion of Surtees as a fellow news gatherer and disseminator. The animosity dated from the

moment on Sunday when Surtees had led the Inspector
into his private room and shut the door on her. This was
not her idea of below-stairs honour. Therefore, glad to
have had her revenge, she was content to have Wiggens
sitting at her side, and gave the inspector to understand
that with the two of them to represent servant opinion, he
wouldn't go far wrong.

'I suppose you would hear a lot of what goes on in the
house, here, wouldn't you now?' Meredith asked, his
voice oozing celtic charm.

'Not much escapes us,' said Mrs Moxon complacently.

Wiggens nodded: 'What she doesn't hear of inside, I do
out,' he said.

'That's splendid, then,' said Meredith. 'Now, I'd like to
hear your opinions of the various members of the household.'

Mrs Moxom blossomed. It was just the sort of question
in which she felt her own sort of informed acuteness would
enable her to shine. 'Well, now,' she said. 'I suppose we
should start at the top. Lady Fairleigh – she's a real lady.
Had a lot to put up with – haven't we all? but her more
than most – but she covers up beautifully, not that it
would deceive a fly. She'd've made someone a very good
wife and mother if she hadn't married Sir Oliver. Then
there's Sir Mark. Well, Wiggens and me are pleased he
got everything.'

'Oh? Why is that?'

'Because the alternatives was worse,' said Mrs Moxon
succinctly. 'There was always this talk about Mark, but I
never saw much harm in him, bar his being full as a fruit-
cake most of the time, and it's not as though the poor
little blighter had much of a childhood.'

'Was it worse for him than for the others?'

'Oh yes, him being the first, and then Miss Bella being
the favourite, and Sir Oliver having exhausted himself a
bit by the time Master Terry grew up, not that he exhausted himself as much as he ought, heaven knows. Well,
where was I, oh yes, then there's Bella – well, I don't

quite know how I'd describe her, more a mixture really. Artful, she is. Knew how to twist her father round her little finger. It used to rile Lady Fairleigh, I know that, though she'd die if she thought she'd shown it. Miss Bella is a bit of a minx, I'd say, but she's not all bad.'

'Not like Terence?'

'Well, I didn't say that, you did, but there have been incidents, it's true – little things . . . I don't like the boy one little bit, and that's the truth. I mind once, years ago, when he can't have been more than ten or eleven, he saw me take a few scraps of food home from this very kitchen for my own tea. I didn't know he'd noticed – he's never been the wide-eyed sort of child – but he watched me for a fortnight, watched everything I did. Then he came along with everything listed neat and tidy in a notebook, and he threatened to tell his father unless I gave him a pound a week. Have you ever heard the like?'

'What did you do?'

'Laughed in his face, what else? I could afford to. Good cooks write their own contracts these days, and Sir Oliver wouldn't dare to give me notice, no more he wouldn't dare say anything to me, lest I gave mine. I spelled it out for him, young as he was. That experience taught him a thing or two about blackmail, I shouldn't wonder.'

'It may very well have done. Well, that's the family. What about Miss Cozzens and John Surtees?'

'She's all right. Keeps herself *to* herself: "I'm not one of you, but I'll be nice as pie if you know your place." She's been very matey these last few days – afraid of missing out on anything, I shouldn't wonder. Now Surtees – ' she thought for a bit, obviously not having expected to be questioned about her fellow servant, and wondering how much loyalty was due to him. Not, it seemed, much. 'Well, he likes money, and he likes power, and that's a fact. No morals either.' Mrs Moxon seemed to swell, as if in consciousness of her own superiority in that respect. Her next words showed that to her (as to the Sunday papers) morals meant sexual morals. 'He likes women, that's no secret, or at any rate, he likes to have women sniffing after him. He thinks he's the cat's whiskers – the prize tom in the neighbourhood, in fact.' She cackled with laughter. 'Thinks more of himself than he thinks of any of them, if you ask me, but there's always plenty of women as will make fools of themselves for a chap like him.'

'Did he and Miss Cozzens sleep together?'

'Miss Cozzens?' Mrs Moxon looked genuinely startled, and her look made Meredith feel he should have used some such phrase as 'were intimate,' rather than his own particular circumlocution. At length she said: 'Not that I know of, no. There's others in the house I wouldn't say the same for.'

'You mean Lady Fairleigh – ?'

There came over Mrs Moxon's plump face a look of the most utter outrage and rebuttal. For once she stuttered for lack of words, a rare experience for her: 'Lady Fairleigh? Why, good heavens, man, you must be out of your mind. I've never heard of such a thing. She's a lady. She'd no more sleep with John Surtees than she would with Wiggens here.'

Wiggens gave a complacent grin, as if some sort of compliment were intended. He had been sitting silent, in an old check shirt dirtied by time rather than labour, so perhaps he was pleased at last to have some real part in the conversation.

'Miss Bella, then.'

'Got it in one. Two, anyway. He talks about it when he's had a few to drink sometimes, gives hints – subtle he probably thinks them, but you'd have to be a half-wit not to understand.'

'Tell me, Mrs Moxon,' said Meredith, turning now to the things that really interested him rather than those which were designed to show off Mrs Moxon's powers as an observer, 'when was it that the rumours of what Sir Mark had said in the Prince Albert at Hadley got to Wycherley?'

Mrs Moxon, intent on being a key witness for the

Crown, sat and pondered, in a real attempt to get at the right answer: 'Well, now, I'd say it was Thursday,' she said, finally. 'Because Thursday's my bread day, and my hands were sticky when I told Lady Fairleigh.'

'It was Thursday when you told me,' said Wiggens eagerly. 'Because that's one of my pub nights, and I mind we chewed it over at the Arms that same day.'

'Then I must have heard from Betty Pratt on my way to work. Her husband had been over Hadley way the night before, and heard it then. I know Surtees went along to Sir Oliver with the story the next day, must have been Friday.'

'Did he always do that?'

' 'Course he did. Sir Oliver used to slip him a fiver now and then, and a tenner if it was something he really wanted to know.'

'Then you don't think anyone in the area would have heard it earlier than Thursday morning.'

'Not they,' said Mrs Moxon confidently. 'If so, they'd have told me. I'm always the first to know. Everyone round here knows I like to hear what's going on. And I'm good about passing it on, aren't I?'

'You are,' confirmed Wiggens sagely.

'So if the poison was put in the decanter by one of the family, or conceivably by one of the servants,' went on Meredith, 'it was likely to be on Thursday or after, if the intention was to incriminate Sir Mark after what he said at Hadley. Is that right?'

Mrs Moxon looked at him with undisguised admiration: 'I call that real logistics,' she said.

The journalistic siege of Wycherley Court went on, and seemed likely to continue until either the case was solved, or some equally sensational happening displaced it from the front page. A little army of ace reporters was now camped outside the gates and along the road into the village: men with faces lobster-pink from the unaccustomed fresh air and sunshine, with beer bellies poking unattractively through shirts with buttons missing, men with an air of living in a paradoxical state of continual excitement and inbred cynicism.

Inside Wycherley Court, the inhabitants withstood the siege as best they could. Bella and Terence were already talking about getting away, but they could hardly leave with decency before a week had gone by. With luck the funeral could be fixed for Friday or Saturday, and then they could take off, to nurse their disappointed expectations in conditions of greater privacy, or solicit the sympathy of friends for their grievances. Meanwhile they sulked and skulked around Wycherley Court, watched Mark gradually assuming the reins of control, and felt their position in the home becoming more and more uncertain. Terence drank.

When Meredith came upon them on Tuesday afternoon it was tea-time, and they were all tucking into shrimp sandwiches, fruit-cake and sponge fingers. The atmosphere was less tense than it had been, at least on the surface: perhaps Mark's revelation of the extent of his knowledge of their activities had had a sobering effect; or perhaps he or his mother had been pointing out to the younger children that a display of family animosities in front of the police was to nobody's benefit, least of all their own.

Meredith's arrival was a signal to Mark to do his duty as host and head of the household. He was getting quite good at it. Meredith was ushered to a seat, and plied with offers of sandwiches and tea. As he let himself be served by Lady Fairleigh, he eyed 'the young master.' Mark was certainly looking better, as well as behaving better: the whites of his eyes were less like pink and red road maps, his suit was now older but more suitable than the sharp job he had been wearing, and his hand, when he passed the teacup, was almost entirely steady. His performance did not please Bella and Terence, but they had been sufficiently brought to heel to keep quiet, and they merely gazed ahead of themselves with an appearance of calm.

'Delicious!' said Meredith, biting a sandwich which was

itself hardly more than bite-sized. 'Now – business, I'm afraid. First of all, I'd like you all to look at these: they're copies of an account Mr Woodstock has prepared of the birthday party here last Saturday night – all very detailed and precise.'

'A preparation for his article for the *Sunday Grub*, I suppose,' said Bella. 'I think he's contemptible.'

Meredith turned to her, his attractive face open and guileless: 'You think you deserved better of him, do you?' he said. For some reason Bella flushed and remained silent. Terence shot a sharp, apprehensive gaze from his dulled eyes in Meredith's direction, but the inspector had merely settled himself back more comfortably in his chair.

'I'd like you all – Sir Mark excepted, of course – to look at his account of the positions around the desk at all stages of the present-opening, and tell me if it agrees with your memory of events. And, of course, his account of the conversations as well.'

They accepted their copies, and waited for him to go on.

'There was one more little thing I was thinking of asking,' he said, still more comfortably settled, and sipping his tea, like an old family friend. 'Could you tell me the name of the secretary Sir Oliver had before Miss Cozzens?'

Meredith's quick, sparkling eye caught their reactions: surprise from Lady Fairleigh, more obvious puzzlement – a creasing of the brow – from her two eldest children, and from Terence, something more positive – alarm, or active dislike, or what?

'Goodness me,' said Eleanor Fairleigh. 'That's a figure from the past. Miss Thorrington – you remember, children?'

Terence grunted and looked down at his plate. Mark and Bella nodded neutrally.

'Could you tell me a bit more about her?' asked Meredith, helping himself to another sandwich and cosifying the atmosphere again.

'Well, let me see: her name was Victoria. I remember that, because she told me she was born on the day the old queen died – that's exactly how she put it: "the old queen." But we always called her "Miss Thorrington," because it's difficult to keep calling people Victoria the whole time, and any abbreviation sounded like *lèse majesté*. She was with us – what? – nine or ten years I should think.'

'And then?'

'Well, she retired. She was about seventy, you see. She went to live somewhere on the South Coast – Hastings, or Bournemouth or Southsea, or somewhere: flats for elderly gentlefolk – you know the kind of thing.'

'You haven't the address?'

'I'm sorry, I haven't. I *had*, because I sent her a card the first Christmas after she left. But there was none back, and I didn't want to embarrass her by going on sending: I thought probably she couldn't afford cards. So we've completely lost touch.'

'Was there any kind of row when she left here?'

Meredith noted that Lady Fairleigh looked troubled, and smoothed her hair distractedly. 'Oh dear – I expect so. There usually was, you know, with . . . with things as they were. I seem to remember she left rather suddenly, before we were expecting it. But what the trouble was I can't remember – if I ever knew. Sometimes I tried *not* to know, you understand, Inspector. Do you remember, children?'

She glanced round at her brood. They all shook their heads.

'Search me,' said Terence. 'I think I was at school.'

'It was some row with Father, I think,' said Mark. 'She went more or less overnight. I don't think we ever knew why.'

'Well, anyway, what you've told me should be helpful,' said Meredith, putting his plate down on a side-table, and standing up. 'If she's alive I should be able to contact her.'

'I really don't see,' said Eleanor Fairleigh, almost to herself, 'what she could possibly have to do with it.'

'I'm assuming,' said Meredith, looking at them in his sly way as he gathered his things together, 'that as the person who typed it, she's one of the few people who knows what's in *Black Widow*.'

He studied their reactions closely. They all looked at him as if he was completely off his head.

CHAPTER XV

BLACK SHEEP

MEREDITH stood by the desk in the study where Oliver Fairleigh, only a few days before, had opened his last birthday presents. He was shuffling together a sheaf of reports on the activities of Mark Fairleigh in the week his father died. They represented a fortune in shoe leather, and would make interesting reading for the car trip. Meredith looked around the study, possibly, he hoped, for the last time: it was not a particularly attractive room, but it was what its owner wanted it to be: dark, substantial, smelling of wealth and social position.

He had made a discovery about the study. One of the bookcases, at the far end by the window, was not a bookcase at all, but a painted wall. He had had excited thoughts about secret passages, but it was no more than another elaborate Oliver Fairleigh joke: with Victorian meticulousness, shelves and books had been painted on the wall, making a perfect *trompe l'oeil*. The books had been lettered in gold, and given titles expressive of Oliver Fairleigh's opinions and sense of humour. They had probably, Meredith guessed, been changed here and there over the years, for the political references ranged from a heavy black book entitled *Merrie England* by Sir Stafford Cripps to a very slim volume (so slim as to be almost invisible) which was entitled *Principle in Politics* and was attributed to Harold Wilson. Elsewhere on the 'shelves' there were *The Mitford Family on Each Other* (twenty-five volumes), and a series of imaginary novels with dreadful punning titles: *From Here to Maternity*, *By Love Depressed*, and, obscurely, *The English Lieutenant's Woman*. The bookcase seemed to Meredith somehow an image of Sir Oliver Fairleigh-Stubbs: ponderous, out-wardly impressive, actually fake, light-weight. He re-membered a description of him by a police colleague who had met him in life: 'a bookie who had wangled an invitation to a Buckingham Palace garden party.'

He had made another discovery in the study, and before he went out into the early sunshine he could not resist the impulse to go back to it once more: it was an elderly dictaphone, stowed away in a cupboard, but reproducing at the flick of a switch with eerie verisimilitude the voice of Oliver Fairleigh a few days before his death – nut-brown, resonant, baritonal, a voice rich in good-living and self-satisfaction: the authentic Fairleigh sound:

' "Flanked in the doorway by two sturdy policemen, the Honourable Jane Buchanan, flushed with shame or fury, turned on her father. 'I did it for love of you,' she shouted. As she walked through the door and out to the waiting sunlight, her head held high, Lord Fernihill, standing by the superb Adam fireplace, let his head fall on his chest and wept bitterly." Do you find that rather melodramatic, Miss Cozzens?'

The reply was indistinguishable.

'No, of course you wouldn't be. And I imagine strong emotion isn't exactly your cup of tea, is it? It embarrasses you, I would imagine. Do you write novels yourself, I wonder, Miss Cozzens, in the secrecy of your boudoir?'

Again a mumbled reply.

'I suspect, you know, they must be very strong-minded novels. Something of the Ivy Compton-Burnett type, I would fancy. A touch of the Doris Lessing. God, how I hate brainy women. Where were we? "And as Inspector

Powys drove back along the stately drive to Everton Lodge . . ." '

Inspector Meredith (not greatly caring for the doings of Inspector Powys) clicked the machine off. Another image of Oliver Fairleigh had surfaced in his mind: talented, perverse, intolerable – Oliver Fairleigh living up to his public image. Was such a man killed merely for his money? A man who had scattered in his wake so many hand-grenades – was none of them lobbed back at his feet?

Inspector Meredith finally closed the study door, and walked slowly out to the stately drive of Wycherley Court. The morning was still very young, and only a few green-horn reporters – those unafflicted by fuggy hangovers or dyspepsia – were already in position at the gate. They were being rewarded by a sight of Bella Fairleigh, wafting past a laburnum tree and along the side of a superb rose-garden. She seemed to have regained every degree of her once habitual cool: with a crisp white coif over her hair, russet blouse and cream skirt nearly to her ankles, she made, in soft focus, the sort of picture Anthony Armstrong-Jones used to take of royalty. With his heart pausing a second in appreciation, Meredith stood by the police-car. By what quirk of genetics had Oliver Fairleigh been able to produce anything as gorgeous as this?

Bella continued, apparently oblivious of the photo-graphers, apparently oblivious of everything around her. But Meredith noted that she was changing her direction, and was willing to bet she would come over to him. Without displaying any obvious signs of registering who he was or why he was there, she did so. Close up, she was very, very beautiful, and as her piquant, pixie face turned up into his, its eyebrows arched in query, Meredith's Welsh heart beat very fast indeed.

'Are you finished with us?' she asked.

'Nearly,' said Meredith. And added: 'Perhaps.'

'You've hardly spoken to me,' said Bella, stating it as a

fact, not a complaint. 'Or Terry.'

'No, I haven't. Beyond getting your account of the positions in the study at the time, and your broad agreement with Mr Woodstock's picture, I haven't felt I needed to. Was I wrong? Is there anything you would like to tell me?'

Bella considered. 'No,' she said. She tilted her head to one side and looked him in the eyes. Meredith decided this must be one of her techniques. The effect was formidable. 'I just thought,' she said eventually, with a little pout, 'that you must have got the idea that I was only interested in Daddy's money.'

'Does it matter to you what I think?'

'Not at all!' She turned away, dissatisfied. But it seemed to matter. Gazing at the ground, she said: 'I loved him. I wanted his money, and I loved him.'

Meredith said: 'Unless it's relevant to the murder, it's no business of mine. It's your brother you have to make your peace with, not us.'

'Oh, Mark! He's contemptible.'

'Has he ever done anything to harm you or Terence?'

'Mark has never done anything positive whatsoever in his life.'

'Except in these last few days, perhaps,' amended Meredith. Bella looked furious. 'On the other hand, you haven't been so guiltless where he is concerned, I would guess.'

'Oh? What do you think I've done to him?'

'Made sure that a good supply of stories about him reached his father.'

A not very pleasant smile crossed Bella's face. She shrugged: 'That's the name of the game.'

'There's something else I think you've done that you're not too proud of, or shouldn't be,' went on Meredith, feeling rather nonconformist. Bella raised her wonderful eyebrows and opened her eyes wide. 'I think you had an agreement with your father. About the Woodstocks.'

'They're contemptible.'

'How pleasant to have so many people beneath your contempt. Are you going to tell me about the agreement? No? Well, I guess that to get your father to be pleasant the whole evening, you volunteered to provide entertainment for him. Am I right?'

'Yes. Why not? We often had little pacts like that. They kept him interested. Poor Daddy was desperately bored.'

'And what exactly did the pact consist of?'

'Why should I tell you?' Bella began to drift off into the garden, but changed her mind and turned back. Meredith guessed that she was at all times desperate to be the centre of attention, and had missed just that sensation since her father died. 'I promised I'd do my best to reduce Ben to a condition of hopeless passion in the course of the evening, and drive that mousey little wife of his emerald with jealousy.'

'What made you think you could?'

'*I can*,' said Bella, formidably, as if her father spoke through her. Then she added: 'I'd met Ben in London, a few months ago. It was just before his wedding, and he was up arranging financial matters. I had the impression the family did some fiddling over death duties, and had more stashed away somewhere than people usually give them credit for. Anyway, he came panting after me like a bedraggled spaniel. It was quite sweet really. Actually I had other fish to fry at the time, but when Daddy told me he'd savaged him the weekend before I thought I'd try and save him from a second attack. So that's all it was. I was going to give him a nice romantic evening – '

'While your father – let me guess – was going to pump little Mrs Woodstock about the family fortunes.' Bella hesitated a moment, then nodded. 'And what was supposed to come out of this little campaign?'

Bella shrugged. 'Nothing. What could? I wasn't going to drag Ben up to my bed before his wife's outraged eyes. Father wasn't going to blackmail the Woodstocks out of their few remaining thousands. It was just something to amuse Father. It was just a game.'

'You both like dangerous games.'

'What other kind is there, worth playing?'

And this time Bella really did drift away, studiedly unconscious of the clicks of cameras at the gate, the morning sun playing on her auburn hair. Meredith dived into the car, punched the back of his driver to waken him from open-mouthed contemplation of the Madison Avenue vision wafting across the lawns, and let himself be driven at top speed through the gates. For once not a camera turned in his direction, and he was grateful.

Safely away from Wycherley, with an hour and a half's drive ahead, Meredith settled himself down in his seat, and began shuffling through the voluminous reports from the men on the beat of the activities of Mark Fairleigh in the week before his father's death. It was, as he had expected, a sort of Drunk's Progress. The beginning and end of these seven days had been within a radius of 30 miles of Wycherley Court, the weekdays in and around London (where he periodically attended some kind of office, or saw people about some kind of orders). But whether in the town or the country, the lunch-times and evenings were a succession of pubs and clubs, often following in a descending curve of respectability as the night wore on. How Mark managed it financially he did not know, but it seemed clear from the reports that fairly little could send him into an agreeable haze, and then the main thing was to keep there. He was better when he had company: when he was alone he tended to drink himself into oblivion or bellicosity.

His progress from place to place in his alcoholic pilgrimage was a vivid commentary on the effectiveness of the breathalyser laws. He invariably drove himself.

The people he met were interesting: they ranged from men and boys like himself – the outcast type, black sheep, shady characters living from one shift to the next and always wanting credit on an expected loan – to petty crooks, con men, gentlemen with a minor racket, people with ways of keeping just within the law, or with manners that appealed to old ladies. In the rich tapestry of the criminal classes, Mark seemed to have stuck to the seedy fringes. Meredith felt he could pick out without too much trouble one of the occasions when Mark was solicited to come in on the drug racket. There was documented a long, agonizing and finally acrimonious conversation in the Walthamstow Three Pigeons late on Friday evening with a man in his mid-twenties – a man with a gaunt, hawkish face, sunken eyes and hook nose. The description exactly corresponded with the bass guitarist of the Wichetty Grub, whose picture on the wall of Terence's room Meredith had slipped in to check up on the day before. He had disliked the face at the time. He had also noted with interest the empty bottles scattered around the room, and the general smell of frowstiness and disappointed hopes.

The other report that Meredith studied with particular interest was that of the clientele of the Prince Albert, that Saturday night ten days before. The frequenters of the Saloon Bar had been only too willing to come forward: there was a long list, with addresses, all of which had been followed up, scattered though they were geographically. The policeman doing the checking up had recorded (with appropriate professional detachment) all the various frills and furbelows on the basic facts which the various witnesses indulged in: 'His eyes were glowing with maniac fury,' young Miss Vanessa Corbett had explained; 'he brandished a table knife in Jack Larkin's face, and then plunged it into the table,' said another romantic soul. The policeman reporting all this allowed himself the luxury of a few exclamation marks in the margin.

But what interested Meredith was mainly who was there at the time – and here the reports were not as satisfactory as he would have liked: they did not, that is, confirm a little guess he had made to himself. But he had often found that people who had a bit to drink could remember much more than they thought, if you could only find the thing to trigger their memories off. He would have, he thought, to find the right sort of trigger. He looked down the list, trying to select the most likely witness for the sort of experiment he had in mind.

It was nearly half past ten by the time they had driven into Wiltshire and found the village of Lorstone. Meredith left both his car and his driver at the little pre-war council house that doubled as a police station. He had seldom found that an ostentatious display of strength had a very positive effect on a witness, and he certainly didn't think it would have one on the witness he was going to interview now. He would, he told the local constable, walk to the cottage, if he would be so kind as to direct him.

It was only a few minutes' walk, and Meredith paused by a tree unseen to look at the cottage before he went up to the door. It was very unlike the Woodstocks' tarted-up little pair of labourers' dwellings. It was a single, one-storied cottage, and – as Meredith had guessed from the newspaper photograph – in a very dilapidated condition. The gate was swinging open on its hinges, the garden was a tangle of weeds and sprawling bushes, the roof lacked slates. If Ben Woodstock was the aspirant man of letters at the beginning of his career, with a cottage to match, this hovel was the mirror of such a career as it coughed and wheezed its way to a dispirited close.

As he watched, the owner came out. He locked the door, clumsily, as if it was not something he was used to doing, then he pottered along towards the front gate. Meredith looked at his watch. It was a couple of minutes to opening time.

Darcy Howard, when he came towards Meredith, looked no more impressive than he had in the newspaper picture: if the remains of an aristocratic manner were there at all, it was in so wispy and wraith-like a state as only to highlight the other dominant impressions to be gained from the man's face and clothes. Darcy Howard was not quite clean, and his clothes smelled of tobacco and tap-rooms. His walk was a shuffle, and he looked around with a sort of roguish furtiveness, as if for acquaintances who could still be touched for fifty pence. Underneath the general air of decay and seediness there was a little spark of light in his shifty eye. Meredith guessed he knew the reason: today, a rare occurrence, he had money in his pocket and another little nest egg in his cottage, and it came from Fleet Street.

He slipped out into Darcy Howard's path. 'I'd like to talk to you,' he said.

'Oh, would you?' Darcy Howard's face achieved something close to a cheeky schoolboy's smirk: he really was pleased with himself. 'Well, you'd better tell me what's it worth to you, hadn't you? People have to buy my time these days.'

Meredith pulled out his identification card. Howard peered at it, snuffling gently with disappointment. 'I've got a half of gin in my pocket,' said Meredith, patting it. Darcy Howard looked wistfully in the direction of the local and sighed. But, apparently deciding that a free drink ought to take precedence over a bought one – one of the few principles held fast to in these last decades of his life – eventually he turned and led the way back to his cottage.

'Bit of a mess in here,' he said, in perfunctory apology. 'The woman hasn't been in.'

No woman would want to. The place was a smelly slum. Meredith sat down on a rickety wooden chair. 'I'm following up that article you did for the *Clarion*,' he said.

'Got paid for that,' said Darcy Howard, baring his old teeth in a great chuckle of self-satisfaction. 'Well, too.'

'It was extremely interesting,' said Meredith diplomatically. 'But of course you had to feed them some of the usual good stories – the Oliver Fairleigh routine. I thought we might get a little closer to what he actually was like at the time you knew him.'

Darcy Howard digested this slowly, and then looked at Meredith in his cunning, bloodshot way. 'Of course, you give them what they want,' he said, grandly general. 'You don't tell the whole truth. You lot do the same, don't you? "The police are following up certain leads which they are convinced . . ." sounds better than "The police are thrashing around in the dark." The newspapers wanted the usual routine, so I dredged up a few stories. Made up one of them myself. It's natural. Especially as there was money involved.' Darcy Howard cast his eye significantly around his unattractive little piece of real estate. Then for the first time he looked Meredith straight in the eye: 'You said you had a half of gin,' he said.

With a sigh which said that he had hoped the interview might be conducted with more of an eye to police standing orders, Meredith took out the bottle, and Darcy Howard jumped up with something close to alacrity and got two smeary glasses and a milk-jug of water. Meredith made his a small one, but Darcy Howard didn't.

'The point is really,' said Meredith, sipping warily, 'that from your point of view you knew Oliver Fairleigh at the wrong time, didn't you? It was only later in life that he developed this . . . personality that so fascinated everybody and you didn't in fact have much contact with him in later years, did you?'

'Not a great deal,' said Darcy Howard.

'Not much after his marriage, I gathered.'

'Oh, we met, of course. But not a great deal, as I say.'

'That was odd, wasn't it? In view of the fact that he married your – what – niece?'

'Not so odd. Eleanor comes from the respectable side of the family. Nice people, but stiff, you know. I was always the black sheep. They met at my place. Not here – ' he gestured round, again, as if to imply that even he would not sink to inviting his niece to such a dump – 'in London. After the war. Anyway, they married. Good catch for Oliver. But they hadn't much use for me after that. Oliver decided to become a country gentleman. I'd served my turn.'

'So you knew him mostly in the 'thirties and during the war?'

'That's it,' said Darcy, apparently relieved that the

clock had been turned back to the period before his casting-off. 'Bright boy he was then. Up and coming. So was I. More than that. I had talent, by God I had.' He gestured towards the rough shelf full of books in the corner. 'Anthologies. Poetry of the 'thirties. There's hardly one of those that hasn't one of mine in it. Worth a mint of money today, some of those books.' His tone was as unconvinced as Meredith felt it ought to be. However he forbore to ask what went wrong. Lack of fulfilment is doubtless as painful to the untalented as to the talented. He just said: 'Of course, Oliver Fairleigh was a Socialist at that time . . .'

'Of course he was. We all were. All the bright boys. He had it worse than some. You'll find that when the old families go in for Socialism – ' he turned his profile in Meredith's direction, as if it were distinguished enough to be stamped on coin of the realm – 'we do it with a bit of *style*, we keep our sense of proportion. Now Oliver, he was what I'd call industrial aristocracy, and when they get it, they tend to go the whole hog. Like Mr Benn, you know. Trade union banners in the living-room and eternal thick mugs of strong tea. Not a bit of discretion, had Oliver, no sense of the ridiculous. Which was as well,' he added, with Olympian spite, 'because he was ridiculous much of the time.'

'So he was very committed in the 'thirties, was he?'

'Oh yes – the Peace Pledge, Republican Spain, Jarrow marches – the lot.'

'When did you notice him changing?' Meredith sensed, so imperceptibly he couldn't be sure it was so, a slight stiffening in Darcy Howard.

'Well, of course we lost touch, naturally,' he said, not answering the question but gesturing grandly. 'We had quite a little group going in the 'thirties.' He reeled off a series of names that meant nothing to Meredith. 'We had the same sort of aims as the Auden group, but we were more hetero. Oliver kept in with us, and with them. Funny to think about it now. He was quite good at keeping in with people at that time. Must have been saving himself up.'

'But it was in the war he changed, wasn't it? And you did serve with him, didn't you?'

'If you like to put it that way. We lost touch round about nineteen-forty, when he joined up. Of course I did my bit in different ways. Anyway, we met up in Sicily in 'forty-three, and we kept bumping into each other on and off for the next few years. He was still a Socialist in 'forty-three, or called himself one. But I think the bloom was wearing off, even then.'

'Why?'

Darcy Howard hesitated. 'Well, he was always a drawing-room pinkie, you know. He could throw dogmas and slogans and theories around with the rest of us, but in point of fact he understood very little of them, and as far as contact with the working-class movement was concerned, he hadn't any. He knew nothing whatsoever about it. Well, in the army he met up with the workers.' Darcy Howard once more forced out his wheezy chuckle. 'I think he discovered they didn't know their place. He did some lecturing – on left-wing topics. They didn't accept his opinions as gospel. He didn't like it. He was always opinionated, was our Oliver from Brummagem.' Darcy Howard attempted a Birmingham accent, unwisely. Then he handed his glass over to Meredith to be refilled with the air of a man who is giving value for money, and then settled back with his glass into his chair, as if his side of the conversation were more or less over and he had told everything he knew.

'There was no incident, then, that was crucial to his change of mind?' asked Meredith. Perhaps he let a note of urgency creep into his voice; at any rate he sensed again a slight stiffening in Howard which suggested that he was walking carefully.

'No, no, not that I know of,' he said, sipping his gin. 'As I say, it seemed to have been coming on gradually. There was once – some time in 'forty-four it must have been – he was invalided back home, after Monte Cassino. There wasn't anything much wrong with him. It was really three months' leave to write propaganda pieces on the battle aimed at the popular market (and *that* didn't please our Oliver. He thought he was more of an *Observer* writer, but they'd got his measure). Anyway, he hadn't anywhere much to go. His father was in hospital – mental home, just between ourselves – and there wasn't any other family. I put my London flat at his disposal, but I believe he also spent some time up North – with a private in his regiment he'd struck up some kind of friendship with.' Darcy Howard chuckled again, but uneasily, as if aware that Meredith was looking at him very closely. 'It didn't work out, I believe. That was Oliver's first real taste of working-class life. It only lasted a few days. He told me later he loathed it. Loathed *them*. He never said much about the class struggle after that.' It was clear that Darcy Howard took immense spiteful pleasure from the story. But then he paused, and – as if thinking he'd gone too far – said: 'But as I say, he'd been re-thinking his position for a long time. Oh yes, I'd seen it coming on.'

Meredith looked at the cagey old crook, dissatisfied with the progress of the interview. Howard was giving away just so much, and no more. On the off-chance, he said: 'He had affairs too at this time, didn't he?' Howard opened his eyes quickly, then closed them again.

'Oh, Oliver always had the odd girl in tow, you know. There was always someone or other in the old days back in London. Pretty dire types, mostly – long matted hair and chunky beads, quoting Freud or Stalin or an unholy mixture of the two. Not my style at all, I can tell you. I'm afraid I can't help you there.'

'I meant in Italy,' said Meredith. 'Or perhaps when he was on leave.'

'Couldn't say, old man. You know what it was like then – well, no, you wouldn't – too young – but it *was*.' Seeing Meredith looking at him and perhaps feeling himself that he had been less than clear, he added: 'Well you'd meet up for a couple of days, have a bit of a ball, you know, and then he'd be posted to Rome, and you'd be sent to liaise with Pisa, and you wouldn't see each other for a couple of months. That's how it was. I didn't know anything about Oliver's private life. Didn't concern me. Had a real little Neapolitan spitfire myself at that time. Still get a Christmas card from her. Runs a tourist hotel near Naples. Such is life. I expect Oliver had something of that sort on the side too.'

'You certainly implied that the girl in the picture was –'

'Oh, one does. Have to make a good story for the press boys. Don't remember the girl from Adam – or Eve, rather.'

'But you must have *known* – '

'Good heavens man, why? Oliver was nothing special at that time. Whereas I – ' Darcy Howard smiled with the irony and the sense of the ridiculous that he had also brought to his left-wing politics – 'I was a promising poet.'

The ex-promising poet slid his glass in Meredith's direction. There was on his face a look of considerable self-satisfaction. He had established his story, and was intending to stick to it. If there was more to the relationship that he could tell (and Meredith was sure there was) he would doubtless have told it to the *Daily Clarion*, for money. Unless he could get something on Darcy himself, that was all he was going to be vouchsafed for this interview.

Meredith pushed the half-bottle of gin across the table, and abruptly took his leave. Darcy Howard hid the bottle of gin in the cupboard under the sink, and pottered off to the pub – late but not (these days) unwelcome. He felt he'd had a good morning.

### CHAPTER XVI

## TERMINAL

THE GENERAL HOSPITAL where Miss Thorrington was lay near the sea front, and as the West Indian nurse led Meredith along the corridors of the second floor he could see from the windows elderly couples walking on the promenade, greeting each other reservedly, or sitting in deckchairs on the shingle, contemplating the horizon.

It was in this genteel, old-fashioned community that Miss Thorrington had lived since she left the employ of Oliver Fairleigh, husbanding her limited means and attending to the observances of her religion. It was to the hospital here that she had been brought to die of cancer with such dignity as she could muster and in such haste as she could. She was, the nurse said, not far now from death.

Her little room was hardly more than a cubicle, but Meredith imagined she valued the cramped privacy of it. The nurse drew back the curtains to let the sunlight in, but the old body on the bed did not stir. Meredith studied the face. It was long and strongly marked, the face of a woman of character: it was, in fact, not unlike Lady Fairleigh's, but whereas her face had the unbeautiful individuality which bespoke Family, Miss Thorrington's face only told of firm middle-class principles of duty, reticence and keeping up standards – principles long held and not found to fail. He was not surprised that this woman had stood up to Oliver Fairleigh.

When, after a minute or two, she stirred and opened her eyes, the nurse said very quietly: 'This is Inspector Meredith, Miss Thorrington, come to have a little word with you. I told you about him last night, if you remember.'

Her eyes found it difficult to focus on anything for any

length of time, and after registering Meredith's presence she closed them. But an expression of doubt flitted over her face. 'An inspector. Oh dear. I don't know how lucid I can be. I think you shouldn't really rely on anything I might say. It's the drugs, you know. They make you so unsure of everything.'

'I promise you I won't rely on it,' said Meredith.

'Then get down to it quickly, please. I'm best when I wake. Did she tell me what you wanted? I don't remember.'

'It's about Sir Oliver Fairleigh-Stubbs,' said Meredith, quickly but clearly. 'You were his secretary for nine years, is that right?'

'That's right. I hope there isn't anything wrong at Wycherley Court.'

'Sir Oliver was murdered, last Saturday evening.'

'Dear me. I didn't know. I *try* to keep up with events . . . with the wireless . . . but I must have missed it, or forgotten. Poor Lady Fairleigh.' Something almost like a smile flitted over her face suddenly. 'But how *horribly* appropriate.'

'Do you remember the books you took down and typed while you were his secretary?'

'Oh yes. Or I could – before this. I'm really rather proud of them, as if they were partly mine. I've often discussed them with people here – he's very popular.' A wicked glint appeared in her clouded eyes. 'I *liked* them, you know. It doesn't do to say so, but I *enjoyed* them. I don't like detective stories that pretend to be real novels. And I don't like all those scientific details. "Damn forensic science," he used to say. I think he was right. People liked Oliver Fairleigh because his books were good entertainment, good fun.'

'But did you like him as much as his books?'

'Oh, *he* was another matter,' said Miss Thorrington.

'Did you take down a book called *Black Widow*?'

'Yes, I did. It was the last I did take down. I never got to clean-type it.'

'How did the murder in that one take place?'

'It was nicotine poisoning. I remember quite well because I've told a lot of people here. That's rather naughty, of course, but they were interested, knowing it wouldn't be published till after his death. Someone soaked a cigar in alcohol, and got enough poison to kill someone.'

'What were the circumstances of the murder, do you remember them?'

Miss Thorrington creased her brow with effort. 'I think it was a big businessman was killed, at an important dinner. It may have been the Lord Mayor's Banquet, or something like that. Sir Oliver rather went in for that sort of occasion.'

'Do you remember any more details?' asked Meredith. 'How it was done, who did it?'

'Oh dear. It was very ingenious and not very convincing as I remember it. I think the wife did it, but I couldn't swear. I think it was one of those where it was proved in advance that she couldn't have done it, because she was too far away – at the other end of the table, or not there at all, or something – but then it turned out that she did. But details – no – I'm sorry.'

'That's enormously helpful. Would you like to tell me how it was you didn't come to fair-type it? Why you left Sir Oliver's.'

'I'd *much* rather not say,' said Miss Thorrington, her voice firmer than it had been so far.

'There was no pressure put on you by anyone? No – blackmail, for example?'

'Goodness me, no. I am *not*, Inspector, the sort of person susceptible to blackmail. Whatever can have put that into your mind?'

'It's something that's sort of in the air. I've heard stories about one member of the family.'

'Terry, I suppose.' The voice suddenly lapsed into tiredness. 'Be careful of Terry, Inspector. I liked Mark: he put up with more than a child should have to. Even

Bella, sometimes . . . But Terry . . . Terry was a *wicked* boy.' Then, pulling herself together with an almost physical effort of her frail body, she said: 'That's rambling, Inspector. Ignore that.'

'I will,' said Meredith. 'But I think you should tell me why you left Oliver Fairleigh.'

Miss Thorrington again seemed to be trying bodily to pull herself together. Meredith decided she was one of those people for whom the prime imperative was to do what was right. But the flesh was very, very weak, and its weakness made the decision more difficult. 'Why?' she said, remotely, at last. 'It will have died with him.'

'Perhaps,' said Meredith. 'Will you let me judge? If it is not to the purpose, I promise nothing that you say will go any further.'

'So difficult,' said Miss Thorrington, still, seemingly, a long way off. 'He was a bad man, a cruel, unfeeling one . . . But one owes one's employer loyalty – even after one has left his employ. So I have always felt.' Then, with what little strength she had, she seemed to come to a decision. 'But of course you are right. In a matter like this . . . murder . . . I *must* tell you, in case it should be relevant.' She swallowed, and fingered her coverlet in some distress. 'He liked to shock. To wake people up, hoping they'd make some sort of scene. You must know that by now. Over the years I cultivated . . . indifference. Unshockability they say, nowadays. But then, one day, he had a phone call. He told me to stay . . . deliberately, knowing who it was, and what it would be about. He had that look on his face, as if to say . . . "This will make you sit up." ' The voice, becoming very, very weak, at last faded almost to nothingness as Miss Thorrington sank into the drugged state which is the last blessing of the incurably ill. Meredith bent very close to her lined face, and caught a few more words.

'A woman . . . He said – dreadful things . . . disgraceful . . . "Your bastard" . . . "I've helped you enough" – '

The whispers withered away to nothing. Meredith stood up, drew the curtains to, and respectfully slipped out into the corridor. Down below on the beach the old people sat and slept and strolled, as if life were infinite, and death could be warded off, with care and sensible clothing.

Down once more in the police car, Meredith suppressed his constable's desire to get started, and sat shuffling through the sheaves of reports on Mark Fairleigh's activities. Finally he found the one he wanted – the report on the witnesses of Mark's disgraceful outburst at the Prince Albert, Hadley. It was not a pub Meredith had patronized more than once or twice, having too Welsh a concern for the quality of the beer. He did not know any of the patrons, and he studied their names and the notes on them with great interest. He knew the constable who had done that particular piece of footslogging. PC Thorpe, a bright tom-sparrow of a boy, with a sharp eye and a sense of humour. His reports were not quite the official thing, and all the better for it.

Scanning the list, Meredith noted by the name of one of the bar-proppers the succinct summary 'flabby wind-bag.' He paused, then shook his head. Not quite what he wanted. That type never noticed much – too busy waiting to get their word in. Then his eye caught one of PC Thorpe's inimitable abbreviations: 't.h.l.o.d.' It stood by the name of Mrs Jessie Corbett, and it meant – as Meredith knew from previous reports of the same constable – 'talks the hind leg off a donkey.' That was more the type. She had been in the Prince Albert that night two Saturdays ago now, with her husband, her elderly mother, and her teenage daughter. Just the thing: a family party where everyone had long ago said everything there was to say to each other and could sit back and watch the rest of the customers. He got on to Hadley on his radio phone.

'Tell her,' he said, in an inspired touch, 'I'll meet her

tonight at eight-thirty, at the Prince Albert.'

Mrs Jessie Corbett, unused to going out for a drink
without her husband, settled her substantial self (purple-
rinsed and navy Crimplene suited) behind a table in the
Prince Albert Saloon Bar, fingered her vodka and tonic,
and said: 'Well, this is better than *Softly, Softly*.'

And her round, noticing eyes seemed to say: 'And
you're better-looking than Barlow, and all.'

Chief Inspector Meredith, raising his pint, said:
'Cheers. To you!'

The atmosphere being so effortlessly cosy, Meredith
got straight down to business (wiping the bottled light ale
from his mouth on his sleeve) by asking her about her
family party of two weeks before.

'Well, there was Mum, she usually comes with us of a
Saturday, though George – that's my husband – always
says couldn't we leave her at home, and for all the fun and
laughter we get out of her we might just as well, then
there was George, same as usual, not saying very much,
and then there was Vanessa, that's our youngest, and she
was in a foul mood and all, because she wanted to go to
the disco, and George wasn't having any, says he knows
what they get up to there – though *how* he knows *I* don't –
and says he doesn't want her with a bundle of unwanted
trouble before she's seventeen, though heaven knows
that's how we got married, but perhaps that's what he
means.'

She came to a breathy pause, sipped her vodka and
tonic and looked at Meredith. I'm a very good bargain,
taken all round, she seemed to be saying.

'Now,' he said, 'I want you to tell me exactly what
happened when young Mark Fairleigh threatened his
father. You've probably told it so often by now the odd
little detail has crept in that's not really what you saw.'
Mrs Corbett did not take offence, and her bright wide
eyes told him she understood exactly what he meant. 'I

want to hear just what happened, with no melodramatics. Okay?'

It was a test that Jessie Corbett passed with flying colours. She described Mark rather well ('the sort you wouldn't mind your daughter bringing home, but you'd want to look at a bit if it looked like getting serious'), described the two couples talking at the next table to her ('some people do talk'), described Mark glowering and drinking, and finally erupting unsteadily at the next table, where he and his father were being talked about. There was nothing about manic fury, or brandished knives, or any of the ludicrous details that had crept into other people's versions. It was admirably done – it was the basic version, as Meredith had extracted it from all the variations of the different reports. That was the test. Now came the serious bit.

Meredith led her on to the other customers in the bar. It was also an area that PC Thorpe had been over with her before, but Meredith had the advantage over him of being on the identical spot. He made her place each person she mentioned where they stood, and he forced her to conjure up the expressions on their face, and their reactions to the scene. It was a real exercise in total recall.

'There was that Colonel Redfern, standing at the bar, always here of a Saturday night, and most other nights from what I hear, all paunch and blarney he is, and he was drinking it in (along with the others) because anything for a good story, anything to be the centre of attention, then next to him was Albert Courtle, garage man, bit of a crook like they all are, but quite nice with it, then there was . . .'

And so on, through the pub, from table to table, from group to group around the bar. As she went on, the pictures in her mind's eye became more vivid, and more detailed:

'Then right in the corner, there was a man and his wife, never seen them before, didn't talk much, just sat and drank shorts. Oh yes, then behind them on the bench, didn't remember him before, was a chap on his own, reading the paper – '

'Oh yes,' said Meredith. 'Tell me more about him.'

### CHAPTER XVII

## DEATH COMES AS THE END

ARRIVING AT MACPHERSON'S elegantly decaying Queen Anne offices at eleven o'clock, Inspector Meredith found the Scottish dragon alone in the reception room on the ground floor, and meekly sent his name up to Gerald Simmington.

'He's in conference with Sir Edwin,' said the dragon. 'He would be obliged if you would wait five minutes.'

'Of course, no hurry at all,' said Meredith. Then to pass the time of day (though her expression did not encourage chat for the sake of chat) he said: 'I suppose you're all busy coping with the rush on Oliver Fairleigh's works?'

'Precisely,' said the dragon, her thin lips registering no pleasure. 'Last year's hardback will be top of the best-seller lists on Sunday again. Reprints ordered over the whole range of paperbacks. Talk of one of those all-star films. As if his death improved the quality of his books. I never cease to be surprised by the reading habits of people.' She threw a disapproving emphasis on the last word, as if the reading habits of dogs and cats were more rational and predictable.

'I was talking to Sir Oliver's old secretary yesterday,' said Meredith.

'Oh yes, Miss Thorrington.'

'She confessed to enjoying Sir Oliver's books. She obviously prefers her entertainment to be frankly enjoyable

– doesn't like all these forensic details one gets these days.'

The Edinburgh Terror gave him a look which said that but for Loyalty To The Firm she would have told him what she thought of Miss Thorrington's literary opinions. She turned to go back to her ancient Olivetti, but Meredith said pleasantly:

'I suppose Sir Edwin is worried about the manuscript of the posthumous book?'

'That I couldn't say,' said the dragon.

'It must represent a great deal of money to him,' said Meredith.

'Sir Edwin is a good Scot,' said the dragon. 'He takes what the Lord provides.'

Meredith wondered in how active a sense one should understand the word 'takes'. He scanned the bookcases in the outer office which contained the various publications of Macpherson's – religious, educational and frankly unworthy. He was saved from having to incur the dragon's disapproval of his choice of browsing material by a call from upstairs.

'Mr Simmington will see you now,' said the dragon, as to a tradesman. She took him into the hall-way and gave him precise instructions how to find his office. As he made his way again through the labyrinth of small corridors and disconcerting steps Meredith saw the maze as an indisputably appropriate habitat for a publisher of detective stories. After various sudden blank walls and hairpin turns he came to the door marked 'Gerald Simmington,' knocked and went in.

The room was as neat and characterless as ever, the desk cleared for action, or perhaps abstract speculation, only the covers of the books on the shelves giving a modicum of colour. The only addition was a glass of whisky by Simmington's right hand. Meredith hadn't thought of Simmington as a mid-morning drinker, but doubtless his profession had its rigours and its *longueurs*. The editor of the Golden Dagger series looked as neutral and uninvolved as ever.

'I hear from your receptionist that the sales of Oliver Fairleigh are soaring,' Meredith said pleasantly.

'Incredibly,' said Gerald Simmington smoothly. 'He was always our best seller in the fiction line. Now he's beginning to outstrip the popular religious works.'

'It will compensate Sir Edwin for the loss of *Black Widow* – if it *is* lost.'

'Perhaps,' said Mr Simmington, shaking his head sceptically. 'Does that mean you've given up hope of finding it?'

'No, by no means,' said Meredith. 'If I'm any judge of character it should still be in existence.'

Gerald Simmington gestured him to a low seat by the door, and then, as if saying something he knew sounded naive, asked: 'And if it's found, will it solve Sir Oliver's murder?'

Meredith eased himself back in his chair. 'Not perhaps in the sense you mean,' he said. 'No, I'm afraid Oliver Fairleigh didn't have a literary premonition of his own end, and I don't think it was precisely used as a blueprint. The thing that's always been odd – and which everyone in one way or another has pointed to, whether charitably or otherwise – is that Oliver Fairleigh was a very slapdash writer, especially as far as plotting and scientific detail were concerned. Miss Thorrington – ' he saw a flicker of recognition in Simmington's eyes – 'says he was a fun writer. Miss Cozzens says she doesn't think anyone copying his methods would ever manage to kill anyone. Sir Oliver himself said "Damn forensic medicine." No – all in all, I haven't got too far with the idea that the method, in detail, was copied from the missing book. And as far as I can learn from Miss Thorrington, the actual situation was fairly remote from what actually occurred at Wycherley Court.'

'Fascinating, this,' said Mr Simmington in his bloodless way.

'One is left with the idea that perhaps someone felt that the mere fact of his or her having read it was enough to cast suspicion in his direction, since the method of poisoning – nicotine is decidedly unusual – was gained from Oliver Fairleigh's book.'

'I see,' said Gerald Simmington doubtfully. 'It doesn't seem to narrow the field very much, does it?'

'Oh, the field is enormous,' said Meredith cheerfully. 'Again and again I've come back to the sort of man Oliver Fairleigh was. They sent me a transcript of his broadcast at the BBC – fascinating! He obviously wanted more than anything in the world to shock or annoy as many people as possible. That's evident too from his behaviour at the Woodstocks'. Dreadful and quite unwarranted – and just to get attention to himself. With a man like that the net is inevitably wide.'

'And he must have been enormously difficult to live with,' said Mr Simmington, blinking sympathetically. He had not touched his drink, perhaps fascinated by the conversation, perhaps out of politeness because he felt he could not offer a police officer one.

'Of course, of course, hideously difficult,' said Meredith. 'Though there again, I have a very slight feeling that – how should one put it – his bark was worse than his bite.'

Meredith's diamond-sharp eyes noticed that Mr Simmington wasn't willing to accept this: his eyebrows rose a mere fraction, in polite scepticism. 'Of course, we here are not the best people to say,' he said doubtfully. 'There was no particular reason for him to bite us. But still – '

'Don't get the wrong idea,' said Meredith. 'As soon as one uses a phrase like that, people get the idea you're suggesting that underneath that rough exterior there lurked a heart of gold. Nothing of the sort, of course. I mean precisely what I say. Mostly Oliver Fairleigh's malice, desire for attention, enjoyment of outrage and chaos, exhausted itself in words. If he had created a scene, he was happy. He seldom took it further than that. He behaved appallingly to Mark, but he didn't change his will. He behaved appallingly at the Woodstocks', but he proposed to introduce the young man to Sir Edwin. He –

but that's another matter. Of course, on the surface it would *seem* that those closest to him had the best motive for killing him. But it may well be that his family subconsciously appreciated how much of his awfulness was mere words.'

'You may be right,' said Simmington, still showing scepticism.

'As a matter of fact there are quite a lot of reasons for thinking the immediate family are not necessarily the most likely suspects in this case. If the poison was put into the decanter just before Sir Oliver drank the lakka, why was such a risky method chosen? The family would have had so many better opportunities than that, so many safer ones.'

'Possibly because there were outsiders present . . .' suggested Simmington, very tentatively.

'Only the Woodstocks. It would be a perverse policeman who would suspect them rather than the immediate family. Again, if the idea was to use Mark's outburst at the Prince Albert to make him prime suspect, the poison can surely not have been put in the decanter during the opening of the birthday presents, immediately before the toast. Because by then Mark was out to the world, and likely to be for some time to come. It would have to be done earlier – either earlier in the day (Bella arrived in the morning), or earlier in the week (Terence had been in the house some days).'

'I see,' said Simmington. 'That seems logical.'

Meredith, his eye resting on Simmington's whisky for no reason he could think of, felt he had got into his best expositional style. This was the kind of thing Simmington ought to like.

'Of course, leaving aside Lady Fairleigh (it is difficult to imagine her trying to implicate her eldest son), both Bella and Terence are very tempting, as suspects. Terry especially, perhaps.'

'There have been rumours,' murmured Simmington.

'There is one big factor against him, though. He was –

we are pretty sure – trying to implicate his brother in the drug traffic, with a view to making a big stink that would finally settle his hash as far as his father was concerned. Not a nice young man, Terry, as Miss Thorrington said. Now, he hadn't succeeded in this, but he must surely still have had hopes that he might. He would hardly embark on a further project to involve him in something criminal so soon. More particularly, since the aim was to get Mark cut out of his father's will, he most certainly wouldn't involve him in the killing of his father – that really would be killing the goose that was intended to lay Terence's golden egg! The idea is quite crazy. By and large, neither Terence nor Bella could have wanted Sir Oliver dead until they were quite sure Mark was cut out of the will, and so far there had apparently been no discussion of it in the family, so they certainly couldn't know. Of course it's just possible the dose was not intended to be fatal. But I have the impression that both Terence and Bella would have calculated the dose to a nicety.'

'One comes back to the brute fact that it is Mark who benefits,' said Gerald Simmington. 'Though of course he's impossible.'

'Not *impossible*,' said Meredith. 'Oh, Mark is a wonderful suspect, no doubt about it. Everything perfect except opportunity. Only provide the opportunity, and – bingo! The five-card trick done again to perfection. But I haven't, as yet, found the opportunity. And you know, if I were Mark and my alibi depended on my congenital drunkenness – I don't think I would have sobered up so conspicuously the day after the murder, would you?'

'Not the family, then,' said Simmington.

'I'm a cautious policeman,' said Meredith, 'not Hercule Poirot relying on his little grey cells. Let's say I don't think the family are as good bets as I imagine most outsiders are thinking they are.'

'I confess, I have been thinking along those lines. I do take your point, though.'

'Perhaps the best approach to the whole case,' said

Meredith, his eyes now straying to the colourful dust-jackets on Simmington's shelves, 'is the practical one: who had a chance to poison the decanter? Did those people have a motive? Here again one encounters difficulties. There were two names that sprang to mind in answer to the first question. Unfortunately, the second question then becomes peculiarly difficult. On the surface the answer would seem to be: no motive at all.'

'But you can't accept that?'

'I can't accept it without a bit of background digging. And then again – how far is a *bit* of background digging going to get you? Sir Oliver's life was – how shall I say? – full of incident. I decided the best line to work on was the assumption that a motive for murder is not, as a rule, trivial. If it came from Oliver Fairleigh's past, it would probably be something big – perhaps, therefore, something he wanted to keep quiet, but by the same token very possibly something not irrecoverable, even today.'

'I see, the Ross Macdonald type of plot,' murmured Simmington.

'Something like that,' said Meredith, not quite sure what he was talking about. 'I wanted to bring a few things together: the people who had the most opportunity; the attempt to implicate Mark Fairleigh; the motive; the fact that this seemed, somehow, a haphazard sort of crime – '

'Haphazard?'

'Improvised. More or less spur-of-the-moment. That all along was my impression. Not a murderer of devilish cunning at all – and therefore not one likely to have concocted any infallible plan. The poison did actually kill Sir Oliver, but equally it could well have killed someone else instead. So, anyway, what do I do? I look first of all at my two people with the best opportunity to poison the decanter. I look for a start at Surtees.'

'Surtees?'

'He had the key to the drinks cupboard in the study some minutes before the rest came in, and before Mark went out like a light. Surtees: thirty-eight years old, I found; one marriage in the past; running a nice little business selling information to Sir Oliver and screwing his daughter as a return for doing the same service. Did he have serious designs (as they say) on Bella? If so, he didn't know his girl. Did he kill Sir Oliver assuming Bella was his heir? Possibly, because he *did* think that. But it doesn't seem in character to go quite so far on such a rash assumption. No – unless there was something else in the background waiting to be dug out, one can only say Surtees would have to be a very impulsive, irrational murderer, and this doesn't seem to conform to his type.'

'I see. And – the other?'

'The other, Mr Simmington, is you.'

Meredith let his eyes rest on the man's face. There was no change there whatsoever, not a flicker of fear or chagrin. He remained what he had been since the interview began: a sandy-haired, opaque nonentity.

'I see,' said Gerald Simmington neutrally.

'Opportunity: the Sunday before the actual murder, when you both had liqueurs together. Sir Oliver broadcast it around fairly freely that under doctor's orders he drank liqueurs and spirits only at weekends. You could poison the lakka on Sunday and be fairly certain he would not drink it until the following Saturday.'

'No doubt that is true,' said Gerald Simmington, not departing from his civil-service tones. 'As I explained to you in our previous talk, we were together after dinner for a very short time, and Sir Oliver did not leave the room. However, I quite realize that is merely my own uncorroborated word.'

'Precisely. And you also say that Sir Oliver fetched the typescript of *Murder Upstairs and Downstairs*, all but the last chapters. Miss Cozzens tells me this was after dinner.'

'After dinner, but – oh, I'm sorry, I interrupted you.' He looked at Meredith courteously, his eyes blank of any other expression.

'So, I look into your background. Age – thirty-two. An

Oxford second in nineteen-sixty-seven. Began working for Macpherson's in nineteen-seventy. Unmarried.'

'Not much to tell, I'm afraid,' said Gerald Simmington apologetically.

'I found the age interesting, though,' said Meredith. Mr Simmington had folded his fingers together in his characteristic little pyramid, and was showing no sign of emotion. Once again Meredith found his eyes being caught by the glass of whisky at his right hand. 'Your birthdate – nineteen forty-five – I had already found that rather an interesting period in Oliver Fairleigh's life. So I looked further into your background. Your mother – '

'My mother – ' Mr Simmington's voice, astonishingly, came loud and clear, and he held up his hand in a gesture that was almost commanding. 'I would prefer to talk about my mother myself.'

'Please do,' said Meredith, adopting Simmington's old neutrality.

'My mother was a very remarkable woman. Only I was in a position to understand just *how* remarkable. If she hadn't fallen in the way of Oliver Fairleigh – anyway, as you will be able very easily to find out, she was a working-class girl, born in Bradford. Both her parents were mill-workers. She got to Grammar School, then to Domestic Science College. She had been there two years in nineteen-forty, but she joined up. She was with the ATS in Italy when she met up with Oliver Fairleigh in late nineteen-forty-three. He'd been lecturing – wonderfully ironic – on 'Towards A Classless Post-War Britain.' She asked a question, and they talked afterwards. They became friends, then lovers. They intended to get married as soon as the war ended – or she did. She did.'

Gerald Simmington's voice, which had been strong and convincing, faded into silence for a moment. But his whole manner had lost its air of apology and withdrawal – as if he were emerging blessedly into life after long years of hibernation. He took a breath, then went on:

'I don't suppose he ever intended it – marriage, I mean.

At any rate, if he did, it didn't survive his visit to her home, my grandparents' home. He had leave in 'forty-four, to write about the Italian campaign. She wangled leave at the same time, and they were together in London. I don't think things were going too well between them even then. Then they went to Bradford. My grandfather was a fine man, an original. He was a mill-worker through and through – a Trade Union man, a Labour Party man. He had his views, he argued them, he never pulled his punches. He hated drawing-room radicals. He and Oliver Fairleigh loathed each other on sight. In fact, Oliver Fairleigh loathed everything about working-class life – the town, the food, the matiness, the manners. My mother said those days in Bradford – it was as if he were being physically sick every minute of the day.'

'And that was the end of the relationship?'

'Yes. They quarrelled. He'd been looking for an excuse for leaving. She was already pregnant, but she didn't tell him until later, till just before I was born. By then things were changing with him. The war was all but over, he'd had his first book accepted, he had changed his politics and was even looking for a constituency to adopt him, though none of the local Conservative Associations could stomach his swift conversion, so he didn't get one at that time. Anyway, he and my mother came to a financial arrangement, and he was rid of us both. I imagine very few apart from him and my mother knew about the episode at all.'

'I rather think someone called Darcy Howard knew,' said Meredith, 'and made a little bit out of Oliver Fairleigh as a reward for keeping his knowledge to himself.' He had noticed a flicker of recognition at the mention of the name, and decided that Darcy had already begun negotiations designed to continue his subsidy. At his age, presumably, one could afford to live a bit dangerously.

'That, anyway, was what happened,' said Gerald Simmington. 'I suppose it was a common enough sort of episode at the time.'

'Why do you bear such a grudge, then?'

Gerald Simmington looked quite steadily at Meredith. 'I've not said I bear a grudge. I'm telling you about my mother. Telling you things you can quite easily find out from others. Well, what more is there? My mother lived for a time with her parents, but it wasn't pleasant – with everyone knowing. And she thought about me growing up. She always thought about me. She was a saint. So we moved to London, where she passed as a war widow. We lived in a shabby area, near Alexandra Palace in fact, and we just about managed on the pittance she got from Fairleigh. It went less and less far as the years went by, of course, but when I began school she could take part-time jobs. There were always extras needed, of course: school uniforms, holidays for me abroad (I was good at languages). Then she might have to ring up Oliver Fairleigh.' His mouth twisted in distaste.

'Was that wise?' asked Meredith.

'Wise? She didn't think of whether it was *wise*. She did it for me. And of course the money always came. As you say, his bark was worse than his bite. But perhaps it would have been better not to have given the money and not to have barked either. She had to put up with – well, you can guess: revolting insults, innuendoes, abuse. He was a hateful bully. When I got to Oxford, of course, I had a grant, and she didn't need to go to him any more. Except once.'

The sharper, newly awakened eyes met Meredith's, and a hand went nervously towards the whisky glass, then drew back. 'Of course, you would know that. That would be easy enough to guess. I was teaching at the time. I'd got a good second, but teaching was about the only thing that seemed open. It was sheer misery, every minute of the day. I don't think there *is* any torture more awful than an incompetent teacher suffers. I was at the end of my tether. My mother rang Oliver Fairleigh and asked if he could get me a job in publishing. With the usual result. Outrage, insult, refusal. But of course in the end he did it –

he got me in here.'

Meredith almost asked if he hadn't been grateful – but he realized at once that this had been the worst thing of all, the ultimate insult: he had had to take help from Oliver Fairleigh; he had put himself in a position where gratitude was in order.

'Two years after that, my mother died. She had over-worked for years, and was not strong. She had influenza which developed into pneumonia, and it carried her off. That is the story of my mother, Inspector.'

'And since he got you in here, your relations with Oliver Fairleigh have been – ?'

'Perfectly normal. When I saw him for the first time he treated me like any other junior employee of the firm. He's gone on doing that – getting perhaps marginally politer as I worked my way up.'

'I suppose it was early on when he gave you the manu-script of *Black Widow*?'

The new, liberated Gerald Simmington – no longer under the pressure of any personal emotion, and seemingly totally relaxed – leant back in his chair, and even grinned broadly. He looked almost happy. Meredith noticed sud-denly that he was quite a large man, and rather a good-looking one.

'Come, come, Inspector. Surely senior police officers don't try to play childish tricks like that. I've told you some facts that you could very easily have found out for yourself – from public records, friends, Sir Edwin. If you wish to believe that I killed my – killed Sir Oliver, that's up to you. I admit no such thing. And I very much doubt whether you could put together any sort of case.'

'At the moment it would be mainly circumstantial,' admitted Meredith. 'Let me tell you, then, how I see the sequence of events. Some of my guesswork will be quite easy to check up on, I think. First of all, you were in the Wycherley area the weekend before the murder, but not necessarily with that intention in mind, not immediately. More or less by chance you happened to be in the Prince

Albert at the time of Mark Fairleigh's outburst.'

'Oh really?' Gerald Simmington raised his eyebrows.

'I have one witness to a "sandy-haired man in the corner, with an evening paper," which I take to be you. I will arrange an identity parade to confirm that – if necessary separate identity parades in which you can be picked out by everyone who was in the pub that night.' Something of the old Gerald Simmington returned in the expression of fastidious distaste that crossed his face at the idea. 'As I say, I think the notion of killing your father was already in your mind, and had been since your mother died. I think hearing Mark Fairleigh threaten his father brought it to the forefront of your thoughts. I think you then rang Wycherley Court and were invited the next night to dinner.'

'I had a standing invitation,' said Gerald Simmington. 'He would always say: "if you're ever down our way . . ." You know how it is. But I knew the sort of pleasure it would give Fairleigh to have his bastard eating at the same table as his wife. He was a connoisseur of that sort of situation.'

'Fine, the picture is emerging,' said Meredith genially. 'You rang, then, said you were in the area and wanted to talk over *Murder Upstairs and Downstairs*, which was overdue. You were invited along to dinner. And you went prepared – with nicotine.'

'Which I just happened to have with me.'

'It's very easy to obtain, as you knew from reading *Black Widow*. Getting it needed no special measures on your part. And of course the victim already suffered from heart trouble, so no great amounts were needed. I think you already knew two things that turned out to be vitally important: Oliver Fairleigh's regime as far as drink was concerned – he was always broadcasting it around – and the fact that his birthday dinner was imminent, an occasion which all the family was accustomed to attend. You confirmed in your conversation that night that

Fairleigh was unlikely to touch liqueurs or spirits between that night and the next Saturday, when all the family would be around. Just before you left you persuaded him to get the completed portion of *Upstairs and Downstairs*, so that you could begin editorial work on it. Did you see the mock bookcase then, with the references to your mother's story? Perhaps. Or perhaps Sir Oliver drew your attention to it himself. Anyway, while he was out you put the nicotine in the lakka. The poison was likely, over a period of time, to discolour it, make it brown, but it is already a deep yellow, and the study is badly lit. Oliver Fairleigh certainly wouldn't notice, and in fact our lab boys, though they *thought* it had been put in some little time before Oliver Fairleigh died, couldn't be sure. It was a very clever piece of work indeed.'

'I'm sure the murderer would be grateful to you for your good opinion,' said Gerald Simmington. 'It rather underlines the fact that so far you have no case whatsoever. Even a poor little editor glutted on garbled detective fiction can see that.'

'I don't think things went *quite* so well for you after that, though,' said Meredith, trying to keep up the tone of unabated geniality which had somehow crept into the conversation. 'Because it was a very hastily decided on murder – hence the feeling I get of improvisation. In that sort of circumstance, little things have a habit of going wrong.'

'Like, for example?'

'Well, like *Black Widow*, notably. I expect when you'd got the poison into the lakka you came home and hugged yourself on your cleverness in using one of Oliver Fairleigh's methods, and obtaining the poison as he told you. And then you thought: now which book of his was it where the nicotine was used and the details given? And you looked along your shelves, and you couldn't find it – and you realized it was in the book that you, and only you had read. Damning!'

'Hardly that, Inspector. Hardly more than mildly corroborative.'

'But it could never be published. Because people would read it, and comment, and the police would look into it. And they would be coming, inevitably, to you – and wondering who you were. Your great strength was how few knew that – not even, I suppose, Sir Edwin. So the book had to be suppressed. It had been given to you just after you started work, after Miss Thorrington left. I suppose you put it in the vaults here, or the Oliver Fairleigh archive.'

'They're chaos, the firm's records,' said Gerald Simmington disapprovingly.

'Luckily. So you got it out, and then had to pretend the manuscript must be at Wycherley. Improvised, you see. A bit last-minute.'

'It would – taking your story as a piece of fiction – have worked quite well if Oliver Fairleigh hadn't left the copyright to his wife.'

'It would have worked only until Sir Edwin started making enquiries about the posthumous work,' corrected Meredith. 'And that would have been soon enough, I dare say. Anyway, this little detail panicked you, and then the plot to incriminate Mark misfired completely because he was so drunk, and then you started thrashing around?'

'Come, come, Inspector, am I the type to thrash around?'

'Well, you did silly things. Like pretending no one here could remember Miss Thorrington's name. I've just ascertained it is perfectly well remembered by the lady downstairs. You even managed to throw a few dark hints in the direction of your employer, though why *he* any more than the family should kill the goose that laid the golden eggs is beyond comprehension. No, it was a good plan, but it needed more care.'

Mr Simmington remained looking at him, still almost insouciant. Meredith's eyes had lost their sparkle. The murderer of Oliver Fairleigh was not going to be the criminal he was most pleased with himself for having caught. He wondered why Simmington did not take a drink, and found his eyes returning to the whisky glass as a fully formed idea suddenly pushed its way to the front of his mind.

'Well,' said Gerald Simmington finally, with a broad smile. 'That's the plot outline. Now perhaps we can get on to the proof.'

'Very little so far, as I say, and mostly circumstantial,' said Meredith. 'But I shall get it. I have a warrant in my pocket to search your flat. I shall search everywhere you've been in the last two weeks, very carefully, I shall get you in the end. No doubt you've destroyed anything you used to get the nicotine. But how did you get it to Wycherley Court? Have you destroyed the clothes you wore that evening?' A flicker crossed Gerald Simmington's face. 'If you haven't there are sure to be traces the lab boys can pick up. There always are. I'd be willing to bet you haven't destroyed *Black Widow*. You're too good a servant of the firm of Macpherson. Habit would die too hard for you to do that. We'll find it. You may find the process slow, but it will be sure.'

'Then I suppose the kindest thing for me to do, Inspector, would be to wish you good day – if not good luck,' said Gerald Simmington, standing. Once more he was the courteous representative of a well-established publishing firm. 'No doubt I shall be hearing from you again.'

But as Meredith began to get up, he seemed to take a sudden decision, and gestured him to sit again.

'One thing I will say,' he went on slowly, 'strictly off the record. I hated my – my *father* – there, I've said it – for what he did to my mother. I loathed him, and everything in me screamed out against the fact that *he* was responsible for *me*. When my mother died, my life was quite empty, quite meaningless. It has been ever since. The only thing that gave it shape, gave it an aim, was the thought of killing him. Thinking of ways to do it, that was a luxury, something that went with my profession.' He gestured at the gaudy, bloody covers dotted on the bookcases round the room. 'But the essential thing, all that mattered, was to kill him. If I did that, there was the victory. If I got away with it, I still had my meaningless life. If I didn't – ' he shrugged – 'what did it matter?'

Gerald Simmington smiled at the inspector.

'I couldn't lose,' he said, and his hand darted to the whisky glass and he drained it down. 'One way or another,' he added, as he lay dying.